The Story Began Once Upon a Time

LARGE AND IN CHARGE

SIOBHAN SMILE

HOSTILE WHISPERS PRESS

Copyright © 2022 by Siobhan Smile & J.M. Dabney

Hostile Whispers Press, LLC

ISBN: 978-1-947184-55-8

Print ISBN: 978-1-947184-56-5

Cover by: Hostile Whispers Designs (J.M. Dabney)

Formatting by: Hostile Whispers Designs (J.M. Dabney)

Editing by: Laura McNellis (AlternativEdits)

Proof Editing by: Kelly Miller

REMEMBER:

This book is a work of fiction. All characters, places, and events are from the author's imagination and should not be confused with fact. Any resemblance to persons, living or dead, events or places, is purely coincidental.

PLEASE BE ADVISED:

This book contains material that is only suitable for mature readers. It may contain scenes of a sexual nature and/or violence.

For my readers who believe like me that everyone is worthy of love, respect and a happily ever after.

The Story Began Once Upon a Time

Odessa

I'd always wanted more. Some fairytale that didn't exist. One day I'd stood up and ran to give my children the life my family and community denied me. All of it had seemed simple in my brain but taking my life back at almost forty wasn't just about changing zip codes. That was until one night in my favorite diner, and the *more* I was looking for asked to sit at my table.

Dani

I was a serial monogamist, but long-term hadn't worked out for me. My fairytale didn't exist. The woman for me wasn't out there waiting, and if she was, I hadn't found her yet. I resigned myself to teaching during the week and playing ball with my friends on the weekend. And then a chance meeting in a diner changed everything. All I had to do was make her see that all the love and support she needed was right in front of her.

Chapter One

ODESSA

The story began with once upon a time. Well, that's what I'd wanted my tale to be, but it hadn't worked out anywhere near that. I'd wanted more from life. In high school, I'd dreamed big. I'd planned to go to college and get out of my small town. Instead, I'd caved to the pressure of my strict parents and married the pastor's son. Over the next twenty years, he'd destroyed me. I was the dutiful wife and mother, waiting on him hand and foot until I didn't even remember my dreams.

Just like all the women in our community, I'd acquiesced to their expectations and lost myself. The older I became, the less I was willing to put up with the treatment. Although I'd accepted my place, I couldn't allow my children to suffer because of my lack of choices.

One day I'd packed up my clothes, the money I'd saved, and got my children in the used car I'd secretly purchased. I'd pulled out of small-town Utah, and I'd lost count of how many times I'd stopped to vomit until we were across the country. Luckily, my high school best friend had assisted me in

1

my escape and gave us a safe place to stay until I could get a job and find an apartment.

A year passed, and although everything wasn't perfect, we were safe. My babies were living a normal life with friends and not worrying about assuming their roles in the community. I hated when my brain flashed back to the time before freedom. Yet I found the more stressed I became, parts of my brain tried to convince me it would be better to go back—safer to return to what I knew most.

"Hey, honey."

I jerked my head up from where I was trying to do my homework from a few night classes I took. A woman, probably a decade younger than me, stood beside my table. She had on a backward baseball cap, baggy t-shirt, and gray sweatpants. She was the tallest woman I'd ever seen.

"You mind if I borrow half your table?"

"Sure." I made room, and the woman slipped the strap of a backpack off her shoulder.

"Thanks. They're slammed tonight. I'm Dani." She held out her hand, and I briefly shook it, taking note of the slight roughness to the pads of her fingers.

"Odessa."

"Thanks again." She removed a laptop and several folders, also a legal pad and pen from her bag.

As she slipped on a pair of glasses, I brought my attention back to my own homework. She ordered food and coffee, and the waitress refilled mine. We didn't speak, just worked in silence as the diner started emptying out around us. I frowned and read the same question for the fifth time.

"Problem?"

"This should be easy. I thought it would be easy. They just said I needed to get the required stuff out of the way before I moved on to the other classes."

"None of that, honey. Show me."

I turned the book around and pointed to the question. In high school, I took all advanced classes and earned a full scholarship before I had to turn it down for the life of the obedient housewife and mother. She tucked her fingertips under my chin to tip my head up.

"Take a deep breath. I can finish grading papers later."

I automatically slid over as she switched sides, and her slimmer body nudged me over. I felt trapped. Her arm was stretched along the back of the booth, and her thigh completely rested against mine. Whatever she was saying was lost in the rush of blood in my ears.

"Panic attacks are nasty things," she whispered almost soothingly and drew strangely calming patterns on my back. "I want you to breathe in to the count of eight, exhale for the same, then seven, six...and so forth. Focus on each breath, inhale through that adorable nose and exhale through..."

I rolled my eyes at her, and she chuckled.

"I'm not the best with boundaries. My mother failed in teaching me personal space."

"My family isn't affectionate."

"You can tell me to back off at any time, no questions asked."

I felt my brows pull together as I saw she kept dropping her gaze to my mouth. As if she noticed, she jerked her attention back to the book. She explained it to me—how to break it down, and praised me as I scribbled on my notebook. She even wrote down a similar problem and had me show my work on that one.

"See, it just takes a bit of practice."

"Thank you. I thought this was easy. I help my kids every night with their homework. I received a full academic scholarship once upon a time."

"You were just getting frustrated and needed a little more time to work it out. How many kids?"

"Four...three boys and one girl, almost sixteen, seventeen and eighteen, my oldest is almost twenty and in college. My baby is the girl."

"You and your husband must be busy." That was an odd tone to her smooth, southern accent.

"No, just me. I'm getting a divorce."

"Starting over's a bitch. My aunt was married for almost thirty years. One day she got tired of his cheating and moved to some tropical island."

"No tropical island for me, just across the country. I really appreciate the help."

"No problem. You shared your table. I teach at the local college."

"What do you teach?" I asked so she wouldn't leave. As much as I loved my kids, it was nice to have a conversation with an adult. My best friend and I hadn't grown apart, but she had a husband, kids, and a full-time job. We caught up every few weeks or months, and it was like time hadn't passed, or we just ignored that our lives had sent us in completely different directions.

"I'm a sociologist. Which means I teach about humans and the shitty things society does."

I laughed, and then I realized she was still surrounding me.

"I was going to be a professional basketball player, but I blew out my knee my junior year."

"Sorry."

"No need to be sorry. I was young and thought I was invincible. Three surgeries proved me wrong. I'm competitive, so I still play. What about you? What do you do when you're not studying?"

"I work as a secretary at a family law firm, spend time with my kids, and take my night classes. Nothing really exciting."

"What about your kids?"

I'd never answered so many questions about myself before.

4

Yet I didn't feel uncomfortable when I answered. "Um, they all have part-time jobs and go to school. I told them I wanted them to focus on school, but with three of them at home, they outvoted me."

"Ganging up on you, huh?"

"Very much. I should get home. Five AM comes early."

"Before you go, if you have any more troubles with homework, you can call me." She scribbled her number on a piece of paper that she tore off her pad and handed to me. "Call any time, even if it's not about homework."

I didn't know how to respond as she brushed her mouth to the corner of mine. I was internally melting down, and she calmly slid out of the booth, gathered her things, and went to pay for her food. I crushed the piece of paper in my fist, and when I went to pay my bill, they told me it was already taken care of.

I tried to focus on her telling me she didn't understand boundaries and that it hadn't meant anything, but I couldn't remember the last time I was kissed. My husband hadn't even done that before he'd push my gown up and climb on top of me. All it did was hurt. And then finally, he'd be done, and I'd lie there staring at the ceiling with my arms crossed over my chest.

The depressing thoughts made me want to cry, and I walked the five blocks to my apartment. We lived on the sixth floor in a two-bedroom place, my boys shared a room, and my daughter and I had the other. Most of the time, I just slept on the couch. I never rested well anyway. Even all those months later, I still waited on the knock that would bring my past to our doorstep.

Everything was quiet as I let myself in. The only light on was the one over the stove. I hung my backpack on the wall next to the three others. I crossed the room to the kitchen to grab something to drink and a covered plate on the counter.

The guilt hit me harder. For two decades, I'd served my family, kept a nice, clean home, and been looked at like the chosen one since the pastor decided I was right for his oldest son. Arranged marriages were normal, but I'd wanted to escape before my time came. That didn't happen; they'd trapped me only days ahead of graduation.

I grabbed a fork and my plate, opened the fridge, and picked a soda. A forbidden thrill filled me as I went to the couch to sit down and turn on the TV. There were so many different things now. My daughter and I could wear pants if we wanted and leave our hair down. We could have sodas and sugar. Their father had deemed a lot of things as frivolous, and that included TV or books not approved by the church.

We'd all had a hard time adjusting to our new reality.

"Hey, Ma." I smiled at Denise as she came around the end of the couch and sat down beside me.

"You should still be asleep."

"Grandma called." She announced as she leaned her head on my shoulder.

"And?" I asked, as once again, I tried not to drive myself crazy over who had given them my number. All the divorce correspondence was handled through our attorneys. One of my bosses, a partner at the firm where I worked, volunteered to help.

"She was asking me and Michael and Gabriel when we were coming home. That your silliness had gone on too long and that you're embarrassing them and Father."

"I'm sorry."

"Quit apologizing. It's different here, but a good different."

"I couldn't do it and—"

"You should've left sooner. He hit you every day."

My appetite fled, my children grew up thinking that a husband could discipline his wife and children however he saw fit. He didn't hide any of it from them, and I just took it. They'd been forced to watch as he took his thick leather razor strap to my back. My sons were ordered to take part. Told they'd need to know how to be the master of the house when they'd be assigned a wife.

"I'm fine, and we're safe here. I promise."

"How was class and studying?"

"I'm too old to be going back to school. Luckily, the diner was full, and someone asked to share my table. They helped me with a problem I was stuck on."

"A male person?"

I laughed at her expectant expression. My children kept telling me I should try to date, but I wasn't ready, nor did I think I ever would be. "No. Her name was Dani. She gave me her number if I had any more questions."

"That's nice of her."

"It was. She said she's a Sociology Professor."

"You should find friends. You can't stay home every night you don't have class and only leave the house for work, school, and errands. I wanted to say goodnight. Eat your dinner and don't worry so much. We're all fine."

She gave me a quick squeeze and a kiss on my cheek then she returned to her room. I picked at my dinner and only finished half before returning it to the fridge to pack for lunch the next day. My gown was hung on the back of the bathroom door. I went to change and got ready for bed.

I used the extra blankets and pillows we kept in a linen closet to make up the couch. Stretching out on the cushions, I stared at the ceiling, and as I started to fall asleep, I remembered the feeling of a stranger's soft lips near mine. The last adult kiss I had was the day I'd married and sold my soul. I blamed the odd shivery feeling in my stomach caused by the kiss on that. One more day and I'd have the weekend off. I needed to catch up on my sleep.

Chapter Two

DANI

I'd never considered myself a stalker, but I'd found myself driving past the diner where I'd met Odessa. When I'd paid for what she'd ordered, they'd used her name and smiled as if they were familiar. I took that as she could be a regular. I've never asked a woman out before who had kids. To be honest, I hadn't asked all that many women out.

My relationships were always brief in nature. I wasn't always good with social clues. The girlfriends I'd had told me I was too much. They said I smothered them. My moms were the type who were loving. Mama pampered Ma, presents and surprise trips—affectionate, and they didn't hide it.

That's what I'd grown up with, and that's what I wanted when I found someone. When we got to the point of talking about the future, kids were always a hard no, and they were iffy on marriage. I drove to the park to meet up with some friends for a basketball game.

I needed a distraction and to stop thinking about a woman I only knew for a few hours. I parked a few rows from the courts, picked up my bag from the passenger seat, and approached the fenced-in courts. My friends weren't there yet, but there was a tall, skinny kid practicing free throws. Each one circled the rim before they'd bounce out.

"You need a lighter touch." I dropped my bag on the clay court beside me.

"What?"

"It's all in the wrist and fingertips." I held out my hand for the ball, and he handed it to me. I dribbled a few times and stepped up to the line, bent my knees, and easily pushed the ball off my fingertips into the perfect arch. "Not everything is about power and strength. It's movement control and focus."

"The guys at school keep talking about going out for sports, and I'm useless."

I wouldn't want to be a teenager again, even if I went back with all the knowledge that I'd learned in my thirty-two years. "Nah, man, everything takes practice. Natural talent is rare. Most people suck at the beginning. Me and some friends are going to be playing shortly. Want to join?"

"Sure. I'd appreciate it. Ma is gonna be by later to pick me up."

"Everyone should be here in fifteen or so. I'm Dani." I held out my hand.

"Michael. I'm more academic than athletic."

"Like I said, it's all about practice and getting the right pointers. There's also nothing wrong with being academically inclined. I'm a college professor who happens to really like sports. Basketball. Baseball. Rugby. Competition is my weakness."

My friends showed up, and we started our game. We gave the boy advice, and by the time he said his mom was there, he'd improved. He even looked proud of himself. I glanced in the direction he was waving and smiled at the familiar figure. *Odessa.*

I followed him as she neared, and I couldn't resist checking out her plump figure in her baggy, demure dress. Unlike the night we met, her hair was loose around her shoulders and flowed almost to her hips. Her freckled face was free of makeup.

"Hey, Ma. This is Dani. She helped me out."

"Hi, Odessa. A little more practice and they'll be begging him to play." I didn't miss the way he stared at her and then me.

"Thank you again. I can't even run without tripping over my feet." Her face turned pink after admitting that.

"We didn't mind helping him out. How's school?"

"Okay. I got an A on my homework."

"I knew you would." I smiled at how proud she looked about acing her homework.

"Maybe Dani can join us for dinner." I darted a glance at him to find him grinning at me. I didn't know how I felt about her son playing matchmaker, but I also wasn't going to turn down an invite if she asked.

"If you don't mind a crowd?"

"Crowds don't bother me. What time?"

"Six?"

"Perfect. Text me the address, and I'll message when I'm on my way. Should I bring something?"

"No, we'll have everything."

"Okay. I'm going to finish my game and head home. I'll see you later."

He took her arm in his and led her to the parking lot. I didn't look away from them until they disappeared.

"Dani, we playing, or are you going to keep staring at your woman?"

I flipped off my friend and jogged back to the court. It was a good thing I could play in my sleep because my head was definitely not in the game. I was too focused on seeing Odessa again. Running into her son had to mean something. I didn't want to get my hopes up, but that didn't mean I wasn't thinking about taking her on a date, just the two of us.

T stopped outside the door of her apartment ten minutes before six and raised my hand to knock. She'd told me I didn't need to bring anything, but I'd stopped at the florist on the way over and picked an over-the-top wildflower bouquet for her.

"Ma, take a breath." I chuckled as I heard a baritone voice on the other side. This one didn't sound like Michael. I knew she had two other sons. The door opened to expose a big guy with glasses with a good start on a beard.

"You must be Dani. I'm Abe." I didn't miss the way he glanced at the flowers and wondered if I'd overstepped.

I entered and then shook the hand he offered. My attention moved past him to find her in the kitchen with the other three.

"Yeah."

"Dinner is almost ready. You can hang your jacket over there."

I laid the bouquet on a small table beside the door to remove my jacket. I felt more than a little overdressed. They were in jeans and t-shirts, but I'd opted for charcoal slacks with a matching jacket, royal blue dress shirt, and a striped silver, gray, and blue tie. I'd wanted to look nice for her. Hell, I didn't even know if she was a lesbian or bisexual. Her shock from my impulsive kiss had been more than just getting one from a stranger. Her being married to a man for at least two decades didn't mean she was straight. But with my luck, she wasn't romantically interested.

I hung my jacket up, retrieved the flowers, and followed him through the small apartment. The place wasn't big enough for five people. Raising four kids, working, and going to school she probably didn't have much left over.

"Hi, Dani." She wore a dress that was a bit more form-fitting. It showed off large breasts, a thick waist, the paunch of her belly, and wide hips. Her hair was in a messy bun, and some of the long strands escaped to hang around her gorgeous face.

"You look beautiful, Odessa." She seemed shocked by my compliment. "Thanks again for the invite, and these are for you."

The way her cheeks turned pink as she took them made me want to buy her more—buy her anything she wanted. I said hi to Michael. Then she introduced me to Gabriel and Denise. Her daughter was a carbon copy of her. I didn't take my attention from Odessa as she found an old pitcher for her flowers and felt my lips pull up at the corners as she carefully arranged them.

I stood to the side as they worked together to finish dinner. They were in perfect sync as they moved around the tiny space of the kitchen. Once they were done, I offered to help set the table. The kids stood on either side behind their chairs. As was my habit, I pulled out a chair for Odessa and Denise. I took the only seat left open at the opposite end from Odessa. Once I sat down, then the boys pulled out their chairs.

They worked in silence to fill and pass plates around until everyone was ready to eat.

"How did you meet Ma?" Michael was the first to break the silence.

"I asked to borrow half of her table at a diner. I wasn't ready to go home and needed to grade papers." I noticed her looking around, and then she started to stand. "Honey, what do you need?"

"I forgot the tea."

"Sit back down. I'll get it." I removed my napkin from my

lap, stood, and went to the fridge to find two pitchers of tea. I grabbed both and set one on the counter near the table. I filled all the kids' glasses and then hers, mine I did last as I retook my seat.

The stares I received weren't easy to ignore. She cleared her throat, and everyone went back to eating. The conversations going on were the usual family catch-up ones, then them asking questions about me. Abe lived on campus, so it was her and the younger ones in the apartment.

Denise worked as a cashier. Gabriel and Abe worked construction. Michael had a job as a short-order cook. They asked about my job, and I told them enough not to bore them. Once we'd had dinner and dessert, I stood up and started clearing the table with her stuff first.

"I can do that." She had her head tipped back, and I had the urge to kiss her plump pink lips.

"You cooked. I can clean."

The boys helped me load the dishwasher and wash and dry what wouldn't fit as she and Denise went to find a movie.

"Thanks for not making her clean up," Abe said as the other two went to join their mother and sister.

"It's polite."

"Dad treated her like a servant. The master of the house eats first. He would've berated her in front of us for the tea. I know it's none of your business, but I wanted you to know what you're up against. No one else probably noticed you're interested in her. We grew up in an ultra-conservative cult-like environment. Men ruled over their homes like tyrants."

"Is that why she's getting a divorce?"

"Yeah, not that Father's going to sign the papers anytime soon. Our grandparents are pushing my siblings hard about Ma giving up her stupidity and coming home where she belongs. She needs friends besides us. Once the movie's over, I'll get you alone time with her."

I smiled as I dried my hands on a towel and folded it to lay neatly beside the sink. I walked into the living room to find the only spot—besides the floor—to sit on was next to her. Michael pointed to it, and I settled in to watch a movie. I relaxed as I slid my arm along the back of the couch and rested my elbow on the arm. I placed my head in my hand and watched her cuddle with her daughter.

With her face free of makeup. Her dresses didn't show off her body. Everything about her screamed innocence when I knew she had to be at least forty; eight years older than me. I knew I was going to have my work cut out for me if I wanted to ask her out. Although, I sensed it would be worth it. First, I wanted to make her my friend. She needed that more than a lover.

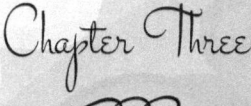

Chapter Three

ODESSA

We were both seated on the couch, and Abe had taken his siblings with him as he normally did on Saturdays to give me privacy. Usually, they went to his dorm for video games and more junk food than I kept in the house. I spent a good portion of the dinner and the rest of the evening trying not to stare. She looked handsome in her dress shirt and tie. She'd rolled up her sleeves to take care of cleaning up.

"Dinner was great. I usually just order takeout or throw in a frozen dinner. Cooking for one is too much trouble. My moms are out of the country for an extended trip, but when they're home, they leave a plate for me in the fridge to this day."

"Moms?"

"Yeah, they met in college. Aggie was out since she came screaming from the womb. Freya, not so much. Freya was every bit the dutiful daughter trying to please parents who demanded perfection. They met during a lecture freshman year. Mama said the best thing about meeting Ma was how easy it was to fluster her. It became her favorite hobby."

I smiled at the way her eyes and face lit up as she talked about her parents. My father was very much like my husband, and my mother was so brainwashed she saw nothing wrong with her treatment. She used to tell me that if I was more obedient, I wouldn't get punished so much. I shook off the thoughts because I didn't want them to ruin the rest of the night.

"Do you mind if I ask if you were adopted?"

"No. They had me the old-fashioned way, well, as old-fashioned as a lesbian couple can. A friend donated some genetic material, and here I am."

"Do you ever think about marriage or kids?" When I asked, I felt her playing with my hair from where her arm was resting along the cushion. We were both turned to the side, but the distance between our legs was safe.

"I used to. I haven't had the greatest luck in the dating department. You know what you grow up with. My parents are very much in love. Mama pampers Ma completely. The more I struck out, the less I looked, I guess."

I didn't know why but I wanted to be honest. My past was shared with my friend and children. Other than that, I'd kept it a secret. If she was going to be around, I'd rather not have her think I was weird. Her opinion mattered. Since I'd met her a few weeks before, I'd thought about her. Every time I'd go to the diner, I'd look up when someone would come in to see if it was her. I didn't understand what the pull was.

"We weren't allowed to date. Marriages were arranged. The first kiss you get is after the pastor introduces you as husband and wife. Start of my senior year, I was informed I was getting married a few weeks after graduation. We were allowed to *court,* which meant we could spend time together with a chaperone...his father or mine."

"Doesn't sound very romantic." She wrinkled her nose.

She had a great face with laugh lines beside her brown eyes.

She had angular features, high cheekbones, and was lean and athletic. Dani looked as if she had control of the world. An overabundance of confidence from being raised by supportive parents. And I was almost forty, still trying to figure out who I was.

"It wasn't. I think someone told my parents about my scholarship. They kept a closer watch on me and informed me I was turning it down. My best friend was going to escape, and I was going with her. I caved under the pressure."

Days of being told over and over that the outside world would destroy me. Detailed descriptions of what the men would do. Raped and murdered, my punishment for being disobedient to God, my father, and my future husband. They'd locked me in a room and mentally tortured me until I felt I had no choice for my own safety.

"Like I said, you know what you grow up with. Sounds like cult behavior, and their success is achieved by being extremely insular communities. Religious ones are even more dangerous. The only way to rule a group of people is with brainwashing. God's wrath and burning in Hell is a great way of scaring followers. It's a systematic breakdown of a person's psyche and free will. It's worse for children born into cults. They grow up not knowing any different. It's a perversion of what religion should be. No matter how long it took you to leave, that took a tremendous amount of courage."

"It was mainly for my children. Abe had already been paired with someone, and they were looking for wives for Michael and Gabriel. Denise was a year away from being told who she'd marry after graduation. I couldn't allow it."

"Like I said, courage." She wrapped a lock of my hair tighter around her finger and gave a gentle tug when I tried to look away.

I wasn't used to the compliments, like when she told me I was beautiful or the way she'd taken care of cleaning up after dinner. My sons had learned to take care of themselves, and when their father wasn't around, they loved helping me in the kitchen or taking care of chores my husband assigned me.

"My kids are adjusting easier than I am, but I know they sometimes question things."

"It takes time. How long has it been?"

"About a year and a half, next month. I'd stolen and hidden money for years. I was allowed an allowance to take care of the house, groceries, and such. If I got new clothes for myself or the kids, I had to write the items down, including the price. So sometimes I put down an extra pair of pants or a new dress. I fibbed on things that he didn't pay attention to. I bought a really cheap car that I hoped would make it. When I got here, I sold it because there was public transport. Eight people in the same apartment for three months until I could afford one for us...I sometimes wonder if I did the right thing."

"Why?"

"I don't know. I'm going to be forty next year. A few more years, all my kids will be in college or have full-time jobs. My kids will be free. I could go back."

"That's not what you want, though. What do you want?"

"I want more."

"More what?"

"I don't know." I sighed and tilted my head. I forced my eyes not to close as her fingertips were massaging my scalp. "I want to finish school. I want my children to be happy."

"What about you being happy, honey? Big world out there. Maybe find someone that wants to spoil and pamper you. Make a list of selfish things just for you."

"I don't know about that. I was married for almost twenty-one years. He was the only man other than my father I was allowed to be alone with. I don't think I'm really prepared to date. But that list of things could be fun."

I'd never even been fully naked in front of my husband before. I'd been plump before birthing four children, some barely a year apart, and my body showed it. My experience with sex wasn't the best either. I hadn't once had an orgasm, and female sexual pleasure was so taboo I'd been terrified of touching myself. The rest of the time, I was too exhausted from taking care of the kids and house that all I'd wanted to do was sleep when I went to bed.

"Doesn't have to be tomorrow or next week, but maybe one day."

"Who knows, maybe."

"I better get going. It's almost"—she checked her watch on her right wrist—"one AM."

I wished she'd stay longer, but I smiled to cover my disappointment. "I'll walk you to the door."

She got up from the couch and held her hand out to me. I took it, and she helped me to my feet. I walked around the opposite end of the couch and met her at the door. She was just getting her jacket and slung it over her arm.

"Thank you for dinner. It was nice to have a sit-down meal with great company." She wrapped her arm around my waist and pulled me in for a hug.

My arms twined around her neck, and I reluctantly let her go as she stepped back to open the door. When I closed it behind her, I didn't know why I was disappointed I didn't get another kiss. Just one on the corner of my mouth like at the diner. I went to the coffee table and picked up our empty glasses to take them to the kitchen.

I made sure everything was turned off and the door was locked before heading to take a shower. Afterward, I'd go to sleep in my twin bed in my daughter's room. I was hoping I'd see Dani again. I still didn't understand why I was so drawn to her, but I felt good when I was with her. And something about that scared me.

Chapter Four

DANI

"Impressionable child in the room." I groaned as I stared at my parents making out at the stove and snorted when they shot me dirty looks.

"If you'd find someone of your own, then you wouldn't have to spend every Saturday night being subjected to me loving on my beautiful wife." Mama shot me another glare, and I coughed to cover my chuckle.

It was always the same. Their suggestions were no longer subtle. At my age, they thought I should be married and settled down, maybe giving them grandchildren. I wanted it. I just kept failing.

"And for your information, I had dinner with a beautiful woman just last Saturday night."

"And we're just now learning of this news?" Ma fought out of her wife's hold to rush to the table.

"You just got back like two hours ago."

"It's modern day. There's phones, email, text, hell, instant messages "

"Her name is Odessa. I met her at a diner one night when

I went in for dinner and a place to work. I asked to share her table because she was sitting alone, and she was adorable. Last Saturday, I ran into her son at the basketball court."

"Fate. And she has kids." Ma nearly squealed, and I had to shake my head.

"She has four, fifteen, seventeen, eighteen, and nineteen. Her oldest is going to college. The eighteen-year-old was accepted for the fall semester." I smiled as I said it. She'd actually called me after Gabriel had told her so she could share the news with me. She'd been so excited. "She works as a secretary at a law firm and goes to school at night."

"Divorced?"

"Working on it. It's complicated. I don't think he wants to sign the papers."

I was curious about her ex. The way he'd treated her and the kids was an abomination. How could anyone look at Odessa and not want to make her happy? I'd studied too many religious cults and fundamentalist communities, so I knew the atrocities they could commit in the name of some God.

Hugging her that night after dinner and our talk had her curved form fitting perfectly in my arms. Her head tucked under my chin. I wanted to kiss her and explore. I'd kept my touch innocent. But for a second, I swore she'd glanced at my mouth when I'd pulled away from her. She found me intriguing, and I was weak enough to indulge her curiosity.

"What's wrong? Talk it out."

"I fear she's straight, and I'm getting obsessed with her. Her marriage was arranged for her before she even graduated high school. She's beautiful and innocent. She's trying to adjust to the outside world, and I don't want her to feel pressured or uneasy around me."

"Dani, you're sweet. You're your mama's child down to the bone. Maybe she needs that pampering and safe space. Who's more capable of doing that than you?"

"I know, Ma, but...my romantic relationships don't give me the best track record."

"Sometimes love doesn't happen on the timetable we'd hope for."

Love happened when the time was right. It was the same thing I'd heard after every breakup. I tried to remember that. As much as I wanted it to happen, there were times when the stars didn't align, or the timing was off. I knew she was right, but that didn't help how much I hated going home to my empty apartment or sleeping in bed alone.

Yeah, I missed the sex part, but a few phones calls or a trip to a club would take care of that. Yet I didn't want to just fuck for the sake of fucking.

"Listen to your Ma. She knows what she's talking about."

I grinned and shook my head. She didn't think her wife did anything wrong. What Ma wanted, she got no matter what.

"I'm hoping."

"All you have to do, Dani, is take your time. Nothing wrong with friends first. Maybe you're not the only one feeling a bit confused, but with her background, you'll have to be patient."

They both pressed kisses to the top of my head and returned to the stove to finish making dinner. I placed my elbow on the table and rested my chin on my palm. Envy wasn't a good look on me. The last few years, I'd focused on my career and friends, and I had to admit I was getting lonely.

I reached across my chest to pick up my phone on the table and scrolled through my texts until I found hers. I tapped out a quick message and hit send.

Dani: *What are you doing?*

We'd exchanged a few texts and calls since I'd left her place but hadn't gotten together. Our schedules just wouldn't line up, but I knew her weekends were for errands and relaxing.

Odessa: *Getting ready to go shopping.*

Dani: *How about I join you?*

Odessa: *You don't know what you're asking for.*

Dani: *Time with you. I'll take my chances.*

She sent me a message asking if I wanted to ride together or if I'd just meet her. I quickly told her I'd pick her up there in thirty minutes.

"I'm out."

"Say hi to her for us."

I waved over my shoulder as I was headed for the door. For a few seconds, I debated going home to change out of my basketball shorts and men's tank, but I shook my head because I didn't want to be late picking her up. I made it across the city in record time and found a spot to park down the block. I jogged to the front of her building and found her waiting for me. She was wearing a cute pink dress that showed a bit more skin than normal and draped her curves just right.

"Baby, I would've come up." I didn't even hesitate to wrap my arms around her to pull her close. "Beautiful as always." I stepped back enough to rest my hands on her hips to be able to get a better look at her.

"Thank you. You're good for my ego." I loved her blushes at my compliments, but I also wanted one day that when I said nice things, it wouldn't make her uncomfortable. "I know, but I've been inside all day."

I turned and offered her my arm as we started down the sidewalk. "What did you do today?"

"Cleaning and laundry. Made shopping lists. What about you?"

"The moms returned from their trip today. I went by for a few minutes. I'd planned to have dinner, but then I'd thought of a better way of spending my Saturday evening."

"Grocery shopping with me was better than dinner with your parents?"

"Definitely." I hit the key fob to unlock the doors and opened the passenger door. I helped her inside and then buckled her in so I knew she was all safe. Her neckline dipped a bit lower and exposed a lot of creamy freckled cleavage.

She shyly smiled at me, and I barely kept myself from giving her a quick kiss, but I reminded myself I needed patience. I closed the door and walked around the front of my SUV, waited for the street to clear out, and got in the driver's seat. As I turned the key in the ignition, I asked her where we were headed. She told me one of the bulk stores for groceries and then one of the super centers for non-food items.

I calculated that I'd have her to myself for hours. "What about dinner before we go shopping?"

"Dinner would be great. The kids are off with Abe to see some new movie. I didn't bother to make dinner just for myself."

We decided on a place to get food, something casual because of what I wore, caught up on our weeks, and I asked what the kids were up to. I kept glancing at her to find her clutching her purse in a white-knuckled grip. I stretched my arm across the console and gently eased her left hand from her purse to lace our fingers. I gave her a quick smile and tried to act natural and that I wasn't thinking about pulling over to kiss her and find out how soft her skin was under my hands like I wanted.

Patience. I could do that. She was worth it. I'd show her how much I cared, and when she was ready, I'd make my intentions known. Hopefully, it worked out like I wanted it. But even if it didn't, I wanted to keep spending time with the beautiful, innocent woman. I'd take a page out of my mama's book and spoil her because she deserved it.

"I was thinking about something we talked about."

I glanced to find her staring at me. "And that would be?" she asked.

"Why don't we make that list? One with all of the things you've always wanted to do. And each weekend, we mark one or two off." I liked that idea. I could have her to myself on the weekends, and I could learn more about how her mind works. As sweet as she was, I also sensed that she held herself back.

"Really?"

"Yeah, we can plan to start next weekend. So you have homework for the upcoming week. Start on that list. I don't care how silly you think it sounds. Write it down."

"I can do that. Like buying myself pants."

"You've never worn pants? Not even since you left?"

"No. Buying dresses actually gives me a lot of options to work with, and I don't need a ton of pieces."

"Okay, pants. What else?"

"Get my hair cut."

"Why the hair?" It would be a crime to cut the silky mass of hair, but that wasn't my choice.

"I've only ever gotten it cut to keep it at my hips, and usually that's only cutting off a few inches. It can grow back, still long enough for a ponytail, though."

"Good choice, that's two things. Anything else?"

"Um, I'll need to think about it. It's been so long...maybe I've never actually done anything just for me."

"I think it's time you try."

"I just spend so much time..." She paused with a heavy sigh.

"Taking care of others?"

She hummed in agreement. "I don't know any other way. When I was sixteen, I swore I was going to break the cycle and get out of town. It took me over twenty years to do that. There's a lot I haven't done."

"Well, honey, anything you want." I pulled into the parking lot of the restaurant.

I was going to enjoy having her to myself, share a meal, and get to know more about her. I'd felt this pull towards her the moment I spotted her in the diner. Perhaps it wouldn't go any further than friends, but I could live with that. As long as I kept telling myself that maybe I'd eventually believe it.

ODESSA

My stomach knotted so hard I felt like I would puke, but I kept staring at Dani's reflection in the mirror as the hairdresser secured the cape. The excitement I'd felt up until that moment was liberating. Dani and I had exchanged messages and calls all week, discussing my list. A break from the rules and expectations of my past, but all I felt was fear.

"Baby, we don't have to do this." Dani closed the short distance between us and came to stand in front of me. She placed her hands on the arm of the chair. "Give us a minute." Her gaze locked on mine as she asked the lady to step away. "You look at me, babygirl. Your hair is beautiful, it's a reflection of you, and it's a remembrance of your past. As much as you felt excited about cutting it, the moment has come. We can give her a nice tip and save this item for another day."

"I"—my voice broke—"I wanted to do this."

"I know you did. And like you said, it's just hair. It'll grow back, but is it something you want to part with? Your list was about finding you...about taking control back. I can't tell you what to do, but I'll support whatever that decision is."

I nodded. "I wanna do it, but would you hold my hand?"

"Of course, I won't let go once, even if I have to sit on your lap when she turns this chair."

"People will think we're crazy."

"Let them think what they want. The only thing important to me is that you're happy."

"You mean that?"

"Every word. Now, should I call her back over, or do we make a run for it and go to the next thing on the list? Clothes. I've been looking forward to you modeling for me all week." As she winked at me, I rolled my eyes.

She was a natural flirt, and as much as I enjoyed it, I wasn't quite used to being the recipient of said flirting. Dani was fun, and I never felt on guard with her. She made me feel safe. Except for that one kiss to the corner of my mouth and a few hugs, she hadn't tried anything. Maybe I'd imagined she was attracted to me.

"And what were you looking forward to?"

"Well, a very short and low-cut dress."

"I don't think I'd have anywhere to wear that."

"I'll find somewhere. So, are we good for the haircut?"

"Yeah, I'm fine. I had my freak-out."

"Hey." She brought her left hand to my cheek and stroked it with the backs of her curled fingers. "It's scary, but I'm so proud of you. Just close your eyes and hold tight to my hand." She smiled as she took my hand and leaned in to brush her lips to the corner of mine. "Just close those beautiful eyes, and when you open them, a brand new you. But this you is gorgeous. I don't think I'll be able to handle it if you get prettier."

"Flatterer."

"Only you." *Close them*, she mouthed, and I obeyed.

I focused on the stroke of her thumb across my knuckles,

and I forced myself to relax as the comb moved through my hair.

"What do you want for dinner tonight? Abe is taking the kids out to the movies, so, just you and me," she said as she occasionally brought my hand to her mouth to kiss the backs of my fingers.

"Surprise me."

"Mmmm, let me think about it. I'll have to come up with something really good to celebrate."

"I may be crying too hard to eat." I joked, but inwardly, I was having a meltdown with every snip of the scissors and tug of the comb.

"You'll love it, I can already tell. Didn't I say you're just going to get prettier, and then you won't have time for lil' ol' me."

She kept her promise during the entire process, never letting go of my hands even when the hairdresser turned the chair, or if she had to shift to stay out of the way. The shorter strands teased my cheeks and neck as the hairdresser styled the finished cut. As time progressed, there seemed to be a shift in the weight on my shoulders—the worry that always existed.

All my doubts of what I'd done since leaving the community. That I hadn't done the right thing. That I'd moved my children from a beautiful house to a too-small apartment, and the worries about affording everything we needed.

"Well, your girlfriend seems impressed. Let's see about you."

"I was impressed before you made a single cut, but now I'm going to have to fight off all the admirers now." Dani's voice sounded different. It still held the same teasing note, but also something else.

I took a couple deep, even breaths, and as I exhaled the last one, I opened my eyes. I barely recognized the woman in the mirror. The straight, heavy mass that had hung to my hips now just touched my shoulders, and waves framed my face.

"I have no idea how you hid those waves, but it's a different woman." Dani circled me until she stood behind me, and I stared at her face in the mirror.

"Was it too much?"

"If you don't like it, give it some time, and it'll be back where it was before. You're beautiful, Odessa, no matter long hair...shaved head, it doesn't matter because the woman right here is just right." She winked at me, and I finally took an easy breath. "Now, to get you a pretty outfit so that I can take you out to dinner."

"Are you dressing up?"

"I have to match energies...gotta get all handsome for my girl. Can't have you getting bored with me."

I shook my head as the cape was removed, and Dani helped me to my feet. We went to the desk, and I paid for my haircut, and then we exited the salon. Once we were on the sidewalk, she laced our fingers. I'd gotten used to her casual displays of affection in the weeks we'd known each other. From what she'd told me about her moms, it seemed to be learned behavior. And I had to admit I soaked up every touch, hug, and soft kiss. It rarely felt as if she was pushing for something.

"Where are we going? Your truck's in the opposite direction."

"There's this shop that some of the ladies in my classes talk about. Affordable, but quality, so I figured we'd take a look. We can start small, a few dresses, couple of pairs of pants and new shirts, and my treat. A present to celebrate."

"I can't let you..."

"Baby, let me do this. It's just a few things, and most of the items on your list had nothing to do with anything you had to spend money on because you have four kids to raise. I want to do this. You paid for your haircut. I want to pay for the rest of the makeover. I refuse to consider it a loan, so get that out of your beautiful head right now."

"How did you know I was thinking about considering it a loan?"

"Because you're independent and proud, you're determined to make a go at your new life. You have a job, you take care of your kids, and you're preparing to make changes to find you. Friends help friends. The fact that we met by accident one night in a diner and then I met your son...it meant fate had a plan. If you want, I'll make a deal with you?"

"And what might that be?"

"Don't sound so suspicious, baby. You're going to hurt my feelings."

"I'm sorry, I didn't assume you were so delicate."

"Smartass."

She made everything fun. In our time hanging out, even the calls or texts, it was as if the pressure melted away. I wasn't expected to be an overworked single mom who existed on little sleep. Until her, I hadn't realized my confidence had grown over the months of being away from my former home. I'd started to look over my shoulder less. While the occasional panic at perceived mistakes hit me at odd times, they'd lessened. I could leave dishes in the sink overnight. I wasn't hyperaware of not keeping the house perfect and being berated.

I hadn't accepted the gradual changes until she made me relax. Yes, my feelings toward my new friend were slightly disconcerting, but I wasn't uncomfortable around her. She made being the new me so easy.

"Thanks," I whispered as we stopped in front of a storefront with mannequins in the window displays.

"For what?" she asked, and I looked up at her.

"The last few weeks, I actually realized that as much as I hadn't felt I'd changed, you made me realize I had."

"In what way?"

"I was so worried about my day-to-day life. Adjusting to being a single mom. To being responsible for everything. Until I'd left, my soon-to-be-ex made all the decisions, took care of all the finances."

"You had a steep learning curve, but you crushed it, Odessa. Yeah, maybe I took you out of the day-to-day stress, gave you a bit of a distraction to allow you to come to terms with the fact you'd already done a lot of the work. The cut and new clothes...they're a physical thing...material proof of the changes you made. So we're just going to make the outside match the mental and emotional changes. Now, I want to see you in a few outfits, and then we can go back to my place for us to shower and dress. I want to show you off."

"Then I better not disappoint." I smiled up at her, and she pinched my chin.

"You could never be a disappointment. I know we don't know each other perfectly yet, but I'm proud to be able to be friends with the woman you are."

"You sure you're single?"

"Perpetually."

"Why?"

"I learned from my mama how to treat my woman. To show her how special she is...pamper her. I don't know any differently. Mama never passes Ma without getting a kiss or a playful ass smack. She makes sure Mama eats before her. She buckles Ma in, opens doors for her. It's very old-fashioned."

"What's so wrong with that? I've never had anyone open a door for me until you. You do notice that you do all those things except the smacks."

"Don't think I haven't been tempted. Let's get to shopping." She made a display of pulling the handle and motioning me in with a bow. "After you, be prepared to be a model. I've been thinking about this all week."

I giggled as she winked and I entered the store. And as I heard the door softly close behind me, she wrapped her arm around my waist. When a sales associate approached to ask if we needed any help, I glanced at Dani.

"My beautiful woman here needs the start of a new wardrobe."

"We have the perfect items. The best way is to buy pieces that you can mix and match but will also work with what you already have. Please follow me."

"You're safe. The only voice that matters is yours. Understand me?"

"Yes."

"Good, let's go see what those sexy legs and hips look like in a pair of jeans."

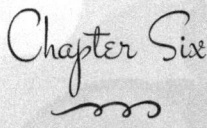

Chapter Six

DANI

"Where the hell is your brain today?" Greta, my former student-turned-teaching assistant, waved her hand in front of my face. "You haven't been this out of it since you dated that wanna-be influencer. Who, might I mention, passed out from that shapewear provided by that company who sponsored her."

"Do you remember all my failed dating history?"

"Yes, yes, I do because when you hit the breakup stage, I have to deal with your spaciness. Please tell me you aren't dating again?" I snorted when she fell to her knees in a prayer pose and batted her lashes at me, which seemed weird from a woman with a cheek piercing, heavily winged eyeliner, and feathered lashes that nearly touched her eyebrows.

"I'm so glad that me being single makes your life so much easier."

"So..." She stretched the single syllable out as she dropped to her butt on the floor. "What's going on? You're barely into your thirties so you're not hitting the mid-life butch crisis."

"Is there even such a thing?"

"Man, if there was, you'd definitely be the one to suffer from it."

"I'm so feeling the love, and I only have a year and a half to go before I can replace you with a more respectful model."

She huffed. "You wouldn't know what to do with a syco-phant who caters to your every whim. Besides, you knew how I was when I was in your class. Your mistake for hiring me."

"That is true."

"So tell me, who is she?"

"Her name's Odessa."

"And?"

"She's almost forty, has four kids, all teenagers, and we've been hanging out as friends for several weeks now."

"But I hear a massive but in this story."

"There's no but. She's not gay or bi. I don't even think she's curious."

"We stay away from the curious ones. They're fickle at best."

"You're very cynical for your age."

"And you're not cynical enough. Do you have any pictures of said beauty?"

I picked up my phone from the desk, unlocked it, and tapped on the gallery. There were a bunch of pictures from our weekend shopping. I'd taken some to text to her kids to show her off since she wouldn't be home until late. We had dinner in a fancy restaurant and went to the diner where we met for dessert. We sat there for hours talking and laughing, and it was the best date I'd had in years. Sad thing was, it hadn't even been labeled a date. I found the selfie we'd taken, my arm across her upper chest, and her hands curled around my forearm.

I handed over the phone and waited for Greta to comment. I'd worried about Odessa at the salon. Some people didn't have a huge attachment to hair, but in some communities and religions, it represented so much. I'd seen her panic. Then at the store, she'd been stiff as she'd tried on form-fitting clothes and dresses shorter than she'd normally wear. Yet as the day progressed, she'd gotten lighter, her smile and laughter freer. I'd even talked her into several more pieces than she was probably comfortable with, but my natural inclination to spoil her had taken over. Every minute I spent with her, I had to remind myself that she'd never be mine to pamper.

I eyed Greta suspiciously as she remained silent. "Okay, you quiet is weird."

"I'm just taking in the gorgeous woman. No wonder you're all over the moon and distracted." She spoke as she swiped through pictures, and I rolled my eyes at her. She didn't understand boundaries any better than me.

"I know. I keep reminding myself she's just my friend. She's amazing, brave and sweet, strong and intelligent, but she's going through a really weird divorce. And I don't want to put extra pressure on her by making my intentions known. She just thinks I'm naturally flirty."

"You never had an issue asking out a woman before. What makes her so different?"

I sighed and leaned back in my desk chair and took my phone as she held it back out to me. "I don't know. The night I met her, I noticed this beautiful woman looking a bit over-whelmed sitting alone by herself. Granted, the diner was packed, but there were places to sit, but I used it as an excuse to introduce myself. Just something in my gut said I had to meet her."

"I'm not one to believe in fate or anything like that, but you see this woman across a room, and you were compelled to be close. Don't get me wrong. I'm not saying that it wasn't meant to be...all I'm trying to tell you is don't spend any more time with her than necessary because you're going to end up getting hurt. I know you. You're going to get attached, and she's going to meet some amazing dude, and go on to have…"

"Don't go there. I already have that thought in my head. And I'm already pretty attached."

"You lesbians."

"Hey, don't stereotype."

"I'm not, and I'm Queer as can be. I just don't understand this imperative to mate. There's so many people in the world and so little time. Hes, hers, and thems. It's like a beautiful buffet."

"Serial monogamist."

"I know you are, and I won't judge you on what I see as a delusion."

"Fuck, how did we ever become friends?"

"Because this place is your life, and if you don't make friends here, you make them nowhere."

"I have plenty of friends."

"Your sporty friends don't count."

"I'll let them know that, in your opinion, mutual interests don't constitute the basis for friendship."

"I'm not taking the bait. As adults, we pare our friend groups down by personality type. We have maybe five core friendships in life. And we always think we're the most non-dysfunctional when we're the most fucked up of the group."

"How have you made it to the age of twenty-one and not tried to overthrow the heteronormative patriarchy?"

"It's a testament to my self-control." I chuckled as she winked at me and kicked my knee with the toe of one of her platform boots. "But seriously, Dani, you like her. Why not feel it out? You always wanted someone who was family-oriented because your moms were. And that smile on her face tells me your presence makes her happy. If you tell anyone I was relationship-positive, I will deny it."

"I'll protect your secret. I just don't know what I want to

do, I don't want to drive her away, but it also hurts to like her and know I have no chance."

"Maybe you have a chance, but you'll never know if you don't ask. With that out of the way, we have this last class, office hours, and then we're outta here for the weekend. Do you have a date with your lady?"

"Sort of."

"Sort of?"

"She grew up in a very conservative community, so she made a list of things she'd always wanted to do. We're going through the list."

"There's your problem," she yelled as she got to her feet and stared at me. "She could have all kinds of feelings that this *community* put in her pretty head were wrong. Repression. Realizing your sexuality later in life is not unheard of. Internalized homophobia is a toxic trait that sometimes takes years to resolve."

"Let's go teach this class. I need a distraction. And I'm the professor. I don't need lectures from you."

"You need all the lectures, Prof, because you have no common sense when it comes to healthy relationships." She grabbed my tie and tugged until I got up. "You're a great catch, Dani. Start seeing that before you lose your chance." She released my tie, and I grabbed my messenger bag and slung it over my shoulder.

I generally didn't do well with advice. I gave it all the time, was told I was good at it but taking my own words of wisdom...not my strong suit. The time I spent with Odessa was the best I'd had in a while. But all I wanted was the best for her, and allowing her to grow and find herself was more important than claiming her as mine.

It was a good thing that I could give these lectures in my sleep, and my classes were more interactive because the next few hours, I existed on autopilot as I finished my day with a few office hours. Mostly freshman students asking for extensions or stuff that could easily be explained if they'd taken the time to make notes. I loved my job, but the first semester was already frustrating. All I wanted to do was pack up and head home. The next day I'd see Odessa, and we'd tackle another thing on her list. She'd told me she'd added a few new items, but she wouldn't tell me during our evening talks.

I adored her more as I felt her confidence strengthen. We healed from trauma in different ways. Shedding the past? That could be something as simple as a new makeover or job. I felt humbled to be along for the journey, but would I be able to let go when she eventually moved on?

Chapter Seven

ODESSA

"Hey, Ma." Abe leaned in the bathroom doorway and smiled as I got ready for Dani to pick me up.

"Hi. I thought you had studying to do tonight? I'm sure you did because I had to listen to your siblings' grumbling about their brother abandoning them."

"I heard this rumor that my mother had a date. Is said date picking you up?"

I rolled my eyes. "Dani has some dinner for her department at work. She asked me to go." I'd had her take me shopping to get something appropriate, and we'd had our first fight as she'd tried to pay for the dress. My nervousness grew over the week as I'd watched video after video on how to do makeup. I dropped my gaze to the black dress that hugged every curve. I'd been more than a little uncomfortable when I'd tried it on, so much so that I hadn't modeled for Dani. Once I'd gotten home, I'd put it back on, and the fluttering in my belly made me smile. My clothes were always baggy and shapeless, but the new wardrobe and dress made me feel good. I was still unsure about how to handle that. Almost forty was a little late to find yourself, but that wasn't something I could do anything about.

"You look pretty."

I glanced at him and then back at my reflection. "Is it okay? Not too much? I watched all these tutorials and..."

"You look great. You've been spending a lot of time with Dani this past month." He crossed his arms over his wide chest, and all I could picture was him at three when he gave me that same stance. It was his stubborn, *I'm going to fight you on everything* pose.

"Is that wrong?" I'd had friends growing up, but whatever this thing was with Dani felt more profound. Not a bad feeling, just oddly comfortable as if I'd known her forever instead of weeks.

"No, nothing wrong at all. You need friends. Father didn't allow you to have any other than us. And I love the new look on you. She's been good for you, Ma. Do you like her?"

"Yes, I like her. She's nice and fun..." I stopped talking as he shook his head.

"I don't mean a friendship like. You do know that you two have been dating, right?"

"That's absurd." My face flushed. Was I that transparent? I'd gone through a few crush meltdowns with my kids, yet, I'd felt I was too old to fall into something silly like that.

"No, it's not." He grinned at me. "Dinner here...she brought you flowers and got dressed up for you. She catered to you over the meal. Every weekend you two get together. I'm not the only one who's noticed."

"Is it making your brothers and sister..."

"Don't even try it. Our world isn't that damn town anymore. You're not under Father's heel. We want you to be happy. And Dani does that. I just don't want you to get hurt. You have no idea what a healthy, non-toxic relationship looks like, and I don't want you to regress and try to talk yourself out of something just because it's not...normal. I told you I was dating someone, right?"

I huffed. "Yes, and you won't introduce them to me."

"I wasn't ready for you to meet him."

I spun on my bare toes and stared way up at him, and the fear in his eyes broke me. "Have your siblings met him?"

"Yes, but not as my boyfriend. He hangs out with us on our movie nights and stuff. He's not exactly happy with me right now because of staying in the closet with my family, and he's dying to meet you."

"Did I make you think..." My voice broke. My children were my everything. To have one of them think that I'd disapprove of anything, especially who they loved, hurt me.

"No. I didn't want to tell you while you were still with Father. I knew what would've happened. He'd cut me off from you, and since you moved here, you'd been working so hard I just kept putting it off."

"Well, I expect a family dinner where he has to attend."

"Done. But I expect Dani to be there, too."

"Maybe what I feel isn't...mutual. Maybe the treatment by your father is making me take Dani's natural flirty nature too seriously."

"No, it's not. Yes, some of it can be your trauma responses. But for the most part, I think you're feeling your first-ever attraction. And said person just happens to be a woman. It's not like anything in your life was very sex-positive."

"And we'll stop there." I held up my hand, and he chuckled. I didn't know anything about sex that wasn't taught by my mother in the lead-up to my wedding. Out of everything, I was terrified of the physical aspects of a relationship.

"All I'm saying, Ma, is that you're on a steep learning curve right now. You've cut your hair. You bought a dress like that." He motioned to the dress. "And you're doing this whole list thing with Dani, something she suggested, and we like this new version of you. You always put everything aside for us and *him*, never thought about yourself, and I love you're being selfish."

"What if...what if it's all in my head and your grandparents or your father finds out?" I couldn't lose my babies, not even for my own happiness.

"Fuck them. They're not important. Finish getting ready. If my siblings come back, I'm going to be here studying. The dorm is crazy tonight. I can't even focus with my earbuds in."

"Well, do what you have to do. Dani's going to be here any time."

"Should I ask her intentions? Where does she see herself in five years? Do I need to chaperone?"

I pushed against his chest and then he grabbed me, hugging me. All my babies were my best friends. They were all I had for almost twenty years. Whether he towered over me and had a beard, he was still my baby—the oldest one who made me a mother.

"No, you don't have to chaperone. Do I need to find you one for you and your boyfriend?" I asked where I tightly hugged his waist.

"As they say, that ship has sailed." He snorted as I pinched his back through his t-shirt. "At least you don't have to worry about being a grandmother by accident."

"There is that. Let me get all my babies off to college and safely into their adulthood before you start throwing grandbabies in the mix."

"Get ready. I'm going to raid the fridge." He let me go and left the tiny space.

I shifted to lean back against the counter and took a deep breath. My children weren't babies anymore. They were adults and young adults who'd adapted and grew up, changed to fit a strange world. I wasn't sure what I was going to do about Dani. But whether it was more or just friends, I enjoyed her company and the way she made me feel as if the person I became fit. I was okay with however it worked out.

The knock spurred me into motion, and I rushed to my room to grab my purse and wrap, slipping my feet into high heels. I'd practiced walking in them all week while the kids were asleep so I wouldn't embarrass myself. Who knew adding inches to your shoes would make you feel as if you were learning to walk for the first time?

As soon as I stepped out of the bedroom, I froze at the sight of Dani and Abe facing off. They mirrored each other with their arms crossed over their chests. And with Dani's height, she was almost as tall as my son. I cleared my throat, and Dani turned her head to look at me and froze.

"Holy shit," she muttered, and Abe choked out a laugh. "We're not going to the party."

"Why? Is it my dress? I don't think I have anything else to wear." I stroked my hand over the curve of my belly and looked down at myself.

"Do I have to remind you about fighting off admirers?"

I waved off the compliment as I realized what she said. "You're biased."

"Every time." She huffed, and I closed the distance between us. "Can't I give you a compliment? Abe tried to talk his way into chaperoning us tonight."

"Of course he did." As I offered my cheek to Dani, I glared at my son. She brushed her soft lips across my skin, and that odd shivery feeling flared in my lower belly.

"He also asked my intentions and then proceeded to menacingly stare at me," she said as she straightened. "My teaching assistant, Greta, isn't going to be any better."

"Great, prepare for interrogation, got it."

"It shouldn't be that bad. She's just nosy. You ready to go? The other kids out?"

"Yes, Abe is studying and has a paper to write. And

came here for quiet and the others are at friends' places for the evening. They said they'd text me if they plan to stay over."

"Either way, have her home at a decent hour." Abe playfully warned.

"Yes, sir." She took my red wrap and draped it over my shoulders, and spread her hand over my lower back.

After I told Abe goodnight, we made our way down to her vehicle, and she opened the door for me. "Are you sure I look fine?"

"You look gorgeous, but more importantly, how do you feel? Confident? Comfortable? Ready to take over the world?"

"I feel confident and comfortable."

"Excellent. The world and other people always have opinions about you, but I want to make sure you walk into that party tonight feeling good." She buckled me in as she spoke, and I once again became distracted by the shape of her smile... the way she looked at me.

I kept telling myself that I was seeing things. Starved for affection by years of being denied, but what experience did I have to measure by? She patted the fleshy curve of my thigh and straightened, closed the door, and I watched her circle the front through the windshield. I was going to have a nice evening, spending time with her and meeting her friends and colleagues. I wouldn't read anything into us hanging out. I needed to work on things, and a possible romance could wait until later.

"What are you doing for Thanksgiving?" she asked as she buckled her own belt and then checked traffic before pulling out.

"This will be the first one with just the kids and I. We were just going to do something small at home."

"The moms were wondering if you'd want to join us? We do this whole Friendsgiving thing. Anyone who doesn't have family to go home gravitates to their home. My moms love having a full house."

"They wouldn't mind five strangers showing up?"

"I've told them about you and the kids. They've been asking for me to bring you by, but I didn't want to scare you off."

"I'd love to meet them."

"I'll let them know then. They always cook enough for an army. Ma lost her family when she came out, so Mama wanted to make up for it. Grew this huge family for her. It didn't make up for the abandonment and betrayal, but it lessened the pain. Having kids, even teens, to spoil will make the holiday easier for Ma."

"She never saw them again?" Was that what my son feared when he'd told me earlier?

"No. She brought Mama to Sunday dinner, and she introduced Mama as her girlfriend, the person she wanted to spend the rest of her life with. They gave her an ultimatum. If she left with Mama, don't bother coming back. She never did. I know she tried shortly after I was born, but they never returned her calls."

"I'm sorry."

"Nothing to be sorry for. It was their decision. Ma was an only child. They lost everything due to their hate. Over thirty years...too long to wait to make amends, in my opinion, but it's what they have to live with. Sorry to bring down the mood."

"I'm the one who asked."

"But you're going through it. You escaped to be free and lost your family in the process."

"No, I still have my children. Once I married, my parents gave me into my husband's ownership. All my mom did after I was married was tell me if I behaved and obeyed..." I jerked my gaze to Dani as she laced her fingers through mine.

"That's not a relationship or partnership. Your person should be equal. Yes, one may be more dominant personality-wise or financially. But when you make a commitment, that person is no less valuable than you. That's what people don't get. Taking your person for granted is the easiest way to lose them."

"Is that what happened with your relationships? They took you for granted?"

"Could be, or maybe I just asked for more than some were willing to give. Doesn't help that my parents are as in love as they were when they met thirty-four years ago. We know what we live. We're given examples and lessons by watching our parents."

"Like me leaving, they learned there were different ways to live."

"Exactly. Denise will know not to settle, and your boys will know how to treat their partners." She gave my hand a squeeze as she pulled onto campus. "Remember, we're here to have fun, and if you're bored at any point, we'll escape. Department heads can be demanding as fuck."

"I'm sure it'll be fine."

Banging on the hood made us jump, and I turned to find a woman lying belly down on the hood with her chin cupped in her hands.

"Were you going to leave me to face this shit alone? Pretty scenery or not, you're in this with me." Her voice was slightly muffled through the glass.

"Greta is harmless...maybe."

"That's your teaching assistant?" I smiled at the woman with piercings in her cheeks who was batting her lashes at lightning speed.

"That's her. I keep saying I'm going to fire her, but she keeps coming back."

Greta tapped the glass in front of me. "You're the one who

has her all heart-eyed and unable to focus." Her wicked grin turned to shock and a squeal as fluid misted the windshield, and the wipers came on.

"Don't listen to her. I swear all the black dye is slowly robbing her of her sense."

"I think I get where her learned behavior came from."

"Babygirl, don't blame that on me." When I rolled my lips between my teeth to hide my grin, she groaned. "We're leaving. I'm not having you hang out with Greta. She'll try to make you her bestie to torment me."

"Out, out, they're waiting for the gifted one."

"Don't listen to a single word she says. I'm coming around to open your door."

"I know the routine."

"Snarky, a new personality trait."

I giggled as she got out with muffled curses, and I turned back to stare at Greta, and I dissolved into laughter as she screamed when Dani dragged her off the hood by her ankles. What had I gotten myself into?

Chapter Eight

DANI

My fingertips gently worked my clit as my body trembled with the ebbing of my orgasm. My chest heaved, and my thighs shook as I lay naked in my bed, the alarm long gone off. Instead of getting up for my morning run, I'd let visions of everything I wanted to do to Odessa circle in my head. I'd thought she was gorgeous in her demure dresses, but when she'd stepped out of her bedroom in the figure-hugging dress, I hadn't been able to breathe.

Masturbation was just something I did every few weeks when I needed to take the edge off...stress relief. Yet since I met Odessa, my normal low-key sex drive increased to where I had to do it every day. When I awakened or in the shower before I got ready for work, my libido in overdrive pushed me toward insanity.

I drew my wet fingertips along the thin strip of pubic hair and over the plane of my flat stomach. I had to get up, I just had to make it through the day, and then I could see my girl that night. Fridays were her homework night, and I'd grade papers so that we'd have the entire weekend free to hang out, work on her list and sometimes have dinner with her kids.

I tightened my stomach muscles and sat up, throwing my legs over the edge of the mattress. I rubbed the scarred skin of my knee as I did my morning pep talk and got to my feet. Shower and then coffee. I was going to need lethal amounts of caffeine.

Quickly I went through my morning routine. I brushed my damp hair back from my face, and then deftly knotted my tie on my way to the kitchen.

My phone rang, and I connected the call. "Waters."

"Hi, I'm not waking you, am I?" The best start to my day was when she called me first thing, but it was a little later than normal.

"No, babygirl, I was just about to make coffee. You okay?"

"Yes, I'm just going to be a little late tonight."

"Anything you need help with?"

"No, meeting with my lawyer after I clock out. He said he had a few updates."

"Well, what time are you going to be here? I can make sure I don't order dinner too early." I didn't push for information about the divorce or if it was close to being a done deal. From what I'd learned about her soon-to-be ex-husband and her parents, they were fighting her every step of the way. She was strong and determined to end the past chapter of her life and move forward. Would they even recognize my girl if they saw her with the new hair and clothes, the light makeup, and a smile that never seemed to fade? I was a witness to the transformation. Some days were harder than others for her to maintain positivity, but there was a thin line between a healthy positive attitude and a toxic one that couldn't be sustained.

"Seven."

"I'll make sure you have food as soon as you get here."

"You're so good to me."

"I try. You on the bus headed to the office?"

"Yes. Power went out overnight, alarms didn't go off, and

most of our phones weren't charged. We were all running around like crazy. Luckily, we didn't oversleep by much. But I didn't get my coffee or breakfast."

"I'll order you something to be delivered. Can't have my girl hungry."

"You don't have to. I can get a coffee and a pastry or something in the breakroom."

"Yes, I know I don't have to, doesn't mean I don't want to. Have we not established that I enjoy spoiling you a bit?"

"A bit, Dani, I think it's more than a bit."

"Perspective. To me, it's a bit, for you, experience warps said perspective."

"Okay, okay, it's too early for a debate, especially when I don't have caffeine in my system. I'll let you finish getting ready for work. A few more stops and my drop-off is right in front of my building."

"Have a good day, babygirl, and I'll see you tonight."

"You, too."

I wanted to call her name and continue the conversation, but I disconnected the call only in order to pull myself back. There was a pattern in my relationships. I was in the pampering stage. It was that one step right before I fell over the precipice into turning things serious. Any other time, I'd be all for it, but she needed me to be her friend, the shoulder to cry or lean on, and I wouldn't take that safety and assurance away from her just for some physical intimacy.

As my phone beeped, I silently cursed as I slammed the top on my travel mug and realized I was going to be late if I didn't leave right then. On the way down in the elevator, I made a quick breakfast order for Odessa to be delivered to her office. I'd done it a few times, so I had her office address saved.

The trip to campus took forever since I left later than usual. I ran through the halls and rushed into my office.

"Wake up earlier for your quickies." Greta barely looked up from her laptop.

"I overslept, I *am* human."

"You haven't been late a day in your life. Your girl has you all mixed up." She closed the lid on her computer. "And after seeing her in that dress at the department mixer, I'm not shocked."

"Quit looking at my girl," I yelled at her as she breezed out of my office.

"Nope," she yelled and popped the P from down the hall.

"I'm getting a new TA." She cackled at my empty threat, and I quickly prepared to get to class, telling myself I wouldn't think about my girl. I was so lying.

Four hours later, I was throwing paperclips at Greta as she kept fucking with me, whispering about asking for Odessa's number. I didn't take her seriously. We were having lunch in my office before my next class, and she was off to one of her post-graduate classes.

"When are you making it official with her?"

"I don't know. I'm already acting like the girlfriend, and as much as I tell myself to pull back, it's not working."

"Maybe I give you too much shit, but on a serious note, I think she's confused about how she feels about you."

I scrubbed my hands over my face. "Is that a good or bad thing?"

"I wouldn't recommend taking too much dating advice from me. My longest relationship lasted six hours and took place between the sheets."

"But you're smart, and I need an opinion. She called me this morning before work. She hadn't had breakfast, so I took it upon myself to order her food and coffee to be delivered. I'm not doing great with adhering to the boundaries I set."

"That's because you, my friend, have no love boundaries. We all have our so-called love languages, and yours is being of service to your partner, pampering them, and also bestowing a lot of physical affection. The night of the mixer, I watched you rein it in, and it was so unnatural."

"She had a shitty marriage. He took her and the kids for granted. He was mentally and…" I stopped and pushed out a sigh as I lifted my arms to lace my fingers at the back of my head.

"You said it was a conservative and almost cult-like community she grew up in, so I inferred that there was some form of abuse. But she looks like she's doing good. Coming into her own. Definitely embracing a less demure dress code. What's holding you back? Her past, her kids, what?"

"Her kids are amazing, independent as hell but extremely close. It's the reason we get weekends to ourselves a lot. Abe takes his siblings to do things on Friday or Saturday nights. Her past makes me cautious but isn't a deterrent to dating her. Maybe it's the fact I want her to do some living…experience things she wasn't allowed to."

"And you don't think probably mind-blowing sex wouldn't be something she'd want to experience?"

I chuckled as she waggled her dark brows. "I try not to think about the sex."

"Oh, you're thinking about the sex. I've seen her. You're definitely thinking about a lot of long, sweaty, nasty nights."

"Thanks, I needed that visual."

"You're welcome."

"Brat."

"I will not deny that. I find it admirable that you want her to have all these things. Find herself in some great spiritual awakening into what real life is, but what about you? How

61

long are you going to hold on being a gentleman? One day you're going to do something impulsive because you're a serial monogamist who believes they found their perfect person."

"Fuck, she is perfect, every inch of her. There isn't anything I don't adore about her."

"Then think seriously about a conversation about dating because"—she stood and slung her backpack strap over her shoulder—"in every way that counts, you're already dating. You're aware of it, but if she's so repressed, maybe she doesn't. Maybe she's having these feelings that she doesn't know how to name."

As she left, I didn't say anything else. She was right. I was dating a beautiful woman, and she wasn't aware of how much I wanted with her. I'd change that. I just needed to get up the courage to open myself to the rejection.

Chapter Nine

ODESSA

I laughed so hard I nearly shot soda from my nose as Dani glared at me from the other end of the couch. We'd started hanging out a few months previously. We'd spent every weekend together, and I'd even spent the night a few times when I knew the kids weren't coming home. When I had homework, I came to her apartment, we'd have dinner, and I'd focus on my assignments while she graded papers or planned her lectures. The last friend I had was in high school, and even then, we weren't worried about the usual teenage things.

Most of us had already been told we'd be married the summer after we graduated. Jenna was the only one who'd escaped our town. Jenna had a husband that treated her like a Queen, and he was nothing like the man who she would've been forced to marry. I'd experienced jealousy those first few months staying with them.

"Let me see what homework you haven't been doing while you laughed at me." She scooted across the couch and lifted my legs over her lap. My stomach felt funny feeling her hands on my bare legs exposed by the short skirt of my dress. I enjoyed pants but was still more comfortable in my dresses. She leaned to the side to stare at my blank page.

Her cheek was only a few inches from my breast, and I tried to ignore what she did to my body. She hadn't tried to kiss me other than those quick cheek ones, but she was free with hugs. When I was with her, I barely had to do anything. She cooked for me. Cleaned. I thought it was like what a normal, healthy relationship was supposed to be. I didn't even care that she was a woman. Being in a big city, me and my children had seen couples of all kinds. I'd even met Lyndon, Abe's boyfriend.

My fear was I was reading things into her actions. She was naturally caring. A few times, she'd talked about ex-girlfriends and how they ended. I didn't understand why, though. To me, she seemed perfect.

"That's an F paper."

"I'll finish it."

She tapped my notebook that rested on my book, and she straightened but didn't move away. Instead, she picked up her legal pad and used my legs to start working. Over the next hour, I finished my math homework and handed it to her to check. I put my things back in my bag and started to get up.

"Where are you going?"

"Home."

"It's Friday, and the kids are all with friends. Abe's on campus with the boyfriend. You can stay longer. I'll make some popcorn, and we'll find a movie."

"I'll make the popcorn while you finish what you're supposed to be doing." I slipped my legs off her lap and started to get up, but I lost my balance. I tried to catch myself but ended up sitting on her lap. "I'm sorry." When I started to get up, she grabbed my hips, and her breath teased my ear. "Am I too heavy?"

"Not even close."

I didn't know what came over me as her lips brushed my neck, and I tipped my head to the side. She sucked at my throat, and I tensed as I felt the hem of my skirt easing up my thighs. The ceiling fan ruffled the fine hairs on my legs. As I started to close my legs, her slender fingers curved over my thighs and stroked higher until the sides of her index fingers nudged my sensitive slit.

"You going to tell me to stop, baby?" Even as she asked, the fingers of her left hand slipped under my plain cotton panties. Her free hand grabbed my ponytail and made me turn my head until she captured my lips in a rough kiss.

I whined as she parted my slit and lightly stroked my clit. My body had a mind of its own. My hips began to arch, and I felt myself grow uncomfortably wet. As she moved her hand lower, two slim fingers stroked into me. I shook as I laid my head back on her shoulder, and she started to tease my aching nipples. The thick, elongated tips tented my bra and dress.

"I bet that pussy tastes sweet as fuck." She didn't sound like herself, and I was shocked when she pushed me away.

My face started to heat with shame, but I didn't have time to escape before she stripped me of my dress and bra, and all that I was left wearing was my panties. I tried yet failed to cover myself as she pushed me onto the couch and stripped off her t-shirt.

I whimpered as her warm skin touched mine and her nipples were as hard as mine, and her breasts were small and firm. I didn't know what to do as she cupped my breasts and pushed them together. Her tongue flicked at the peaks, my back arched violently, and it was too much. I placed my hands on her chest and pushed her up.

"Hey, hey, it's okay, shh, baby, we'll stop." I felt her rest her forearms on the cushion beside my head. Her thumbs wiped at the corners of my eyes, and I realized I was crying. "I'm sorry

I scared you. I'll get up, you can go to the bathroom to wash your face, and I'll get you a car." She placed her forehead on mine and gently kissed me over and over until I calmed.

"He just used to get on top of me, and I'd just lie there with my fingers laced on my chest, waiting for him to be done. I don't know what I'm doing."

"What you felt scared you?"

I nodded, and I squeaked as she relaxed fully on me again, her slim hips holding my thighs open. Her tongue stroked over my lips as her left hand cupped the side of my breast. She gently rolled my nipple with her thumb. A sigh turned to a gasp as the pleasure grew in intensity but slower this time.

"You should be loved on, baby. Kissed. Touched." Her tongue pushed against my lips, and I opened as she tenderly teased my nipples. I lifted my legs to open them wider as she rubbed her belly against my aching slit. I brought my hands to the small of her back and drew my nails up her skin, tracing the shallow indent between her back muscles.

"Can I get you off? Just that, nothing else."

I nodded and fought her a bit when she lifted to throw the back cushions to the floor behind the couch, and then she lifted onto her knees, stretching out beside me. She didn't trap me with her body. I could get up off the couch at any time. Her hand slipped around the inside of my right thigh and lifted it to rest over her legs. I watched her face as she nudged my left thigh until I lowered my foot to the floor and opened myself for her. No one had ever looked at me like that before. Her features were strained, and her cheeks were flushed red. She slipped her left arm under my neck. As I was about to ask her what she was going to do, her mouth was back on mine.

I arched into her touch as she caressed her hand across and around my breasts, squeezed and plucked at my tight nipples. This time I was prepared. I didn't even think about the way my body jiggled as I moved or that my breasts sagged to the sides. Every stretch mark and dimple on display. I'd never been naked in front of anyone in my entire adult life.

By the time she reached the waistband of my panties, my lips felt swollen and sensitive, and I was trembling uncontrollably. She released my mouth and scooted down until she could wrap her full, firm lips around my nipple. She strongly suckled as I brought my left arm across me to comb my fingers through her short, shaggy hair. My head fell back as she filled me again with two fingers, thrusting them in and out, paying close attention to a single spot inside me. I arched my hips up to get more.

"Fuck, you're so hot, tight, so fucking needy."

I was going to ask was that wrong, but her thumb stroking my clit in slow circles emptied my brain of all thoughts or sense. I heard her voice low and husky in my ear as she worked me. My belly felt like it was cramping. Just as I was about to tell her to stop—something was wrong—an intense pleasure bowed my back. My lips parted, and a long groan escaped as I felt myself bear down on her fingers, and my release soaked her hand and my panties.

I think I told her to stop as I tried to close my thighs as it became too much, and then I forced my eyes open just as I saw her shoving her hand into her pants. Her mouth captured mine as I felt her rubbing herself. She was grunting and moaning as she shook, her mouth fell open, and I saw her eyes squeeze shut. She jerked beside me until she collapsed, her mouth finding mine again as she kissed me lazily.

"Was that okay?" she asked as I felt wet fingers stroke my belly and squeeze the fleshy curve. "God, I love how soft you are." She tested every squishy part of my body as she seemed to not be able to stop pressing her lips to mine. "Stay with me tonight, please. I want you to sleep in my bed."

"I shouldn't."

"I won't make you stay. We went a lot farther than I planned, but as soon as I felt you on my lap. I've been thinking about kissing you for real since that tease of one in the diner."

"You really want me?"

"More than anything, all I want is a chance. Maybe take you on a real date. Hang out without work or homework to do. I know this is new. I know it's probably scary because I'm a woman. I can be patient. All I want is for you to give me a chance, or did I ruin it?"

"You didn't ruin it. I'm just...unsure. Not about you or you being a woman, more me. I just need to process."

"Then process, but don't shut me out. That's all I ask."

I wrapped my arms around her neck as she pushed her lips to mine. My face heated as her right hand tugged at my panties as she stroked along my fleshy lower belly.

"Fuck, I can't help touching you." Her lips moved along my cheek to my ear and the sensitive spot behind it. "I dreamed about you naked in my bed. Taking you in every way you'd let me. Please stay. I just want to hold you while I sleep. I'll get you up early enough to be home before the kids. I'd prefer if you didn't leave so late, even if that means I crash on the couch and you take my bed."

"I'll stay, but I'm scared."

"I don't want you scared. I want you to be comfortable and safe with me."

"I do feel safe, but I like you too much. I don't want this to ruin it."

"It won't, I promise. We'll go on romantic dates. We'll spend time with the kids as a couple. It's important that your kids approve."

"Okay, I'll try."

"That's all I ask. Come on. We can get a shower together

and curl up in bed. I'll set the alarm, and then I'll cuddle you. How does that sound?"

"Really good."

I accepted one more kiss before we got off the couch, and I hoped I wasn't about to get hurt.

Chapter Ten

DANI

T he kids approved as I'd hoped. Abe had pulled me
aside and told me they'd talked. Michael had noticed
the day at the courts, and of course, he'd had to play
matchmaker. Abe had upped his weekends with the kids to
give us time together. I should've known. Odessa and I were
about to go on our first real out-in-the-world date. We'd gone
out as friends plenty, but this felt like everything would finally
work out.

After the night in my apartment, I stopped holding back. I
was all-in and wouldn't pretend I wasn't. My end game was
making her mine, becoming a part of her family and her mine.
We were going to my moms' for Thanksgiving next week. Ma
was practically manic over a prospective daughter-in-law with
kids. I'd made Mama promise to pull her back a bit just until
my girl became more comfortable with me.

All I'd thought about all week was waking up with a naked
Odessa cuddled in my arms. The rounded curve of her lower
belly in my hand. I'd memorized every scar and stretch mark,
every beautiful soft roll, and dimple. She'd awakened to find
me watching her sleep, and she'd smiled as she rolled over to

shyly tuck her face against my throat. I'd almost tried talking her into staying the day, but I told her I'd get her home before the kids.

That night I was going to surprise her with another first. I'd called my friend to get my motorcycle out of storage, and I'd told Odessa to wear jeans and a warm shirt. I'd picked her up a faux leather jacket and a pair of boots along with a helmet. It was one of the reasons I loved living in the south the best. The weather was usually good for a ride most of the year. There was a great seafood place about forty minutes away, and we could take a walk on the boardwalk.

I pulled up to the curb and cut the engine, dismounted as I removed my helmet, and made my way inside. The trip to the sixth floor didn't take long, and I stood outside Odessa's door. I raised my hand to knock, and the door flew open.

"Save me." Odessa grabbed me and dragged me inside, the kids were lined up, and my girl's cheeks were bright pink.

"What are you doing to your mother?" I asked as I wrapped my arm around Odessa's waist and leaned down to kiss her cheek.

"We weren't doing nothing," Gabriel answered with an evil grin.

"Double negative implies the positive. You're not meant for a life of crime." I chuckled. I adored all four of them. They were just like their mother. "So spill it?"

"We just asked if we should get her some dental dam..." Denise stared straight at her mother.

I choked off a laugh, but I cleared my throat to cover it as I took in every mischievous expression. "And that is enough internet for you four. No wonder my baby's red." I glanced down at her to find her in a pair of jeans that lovingly hugged her hips and thighs. I'd bet a years' salary the view from the back was just as sexy. "Here, this is for you." I handed her the backpack.

"Dani."

"These are things that you need. Tonight's another first. It wasn't on your list, but I wanted to surprise you. I got my motorcycle out of storage for our date."

"Really?" She grinned and hugged the bag to her chest.

"Yes, really. There's a helmet, a jacket to protect you from the wind, and a pair of boots. Put everything on, and we can go. We have a forty-minute ride ahead of us." I quickly kissed her soft lips, and then she ran over to the couch.

"Where are you taking her?" Abe came to stand beside me and asked quietly.

"There's a seafood place that's right on the water and then a nice walk on the boardwalk, and maybe a few rides and games."

"She's never done any of that."

"I know," I whispered as I watched Odessa remove her shoes and slip on the high-heeled boots that zipped to her knees.

"She's been really happy lately, Dani, and as much shit as we give her, we're all happy about it."

"I want her to have all the experiences...show her the outside world isn't all that scary or overwhelming. What are you doing with the baby siblings tonight?"

"Lyndon and I are getting pizza at his place. We're going to rent some movies and crash there so you two don't have to hurry home. Even though my brothers and sister are old enough to take care of themselves, I know Ma worries about them being alone at night."

"Thanks."

"I spent eighteen years watching a man literally beat my mother down, and she told me to take care of myself because she wanted me to have a chance in the outside world. I'll do anything to have her be able to do the same."

"I'm sorry you had to..." He shook his head to cut me off.

"I know that's standard response is to apologize, but that sorry has to come from the man who caused it, not you."

"You're a lot like your mother."

"She raised us. Father had minimal input. Home and children were the woman's responsibility. God, I don't know how she survived almost thirty-nine years of it."

"When's her birthday? I want to do something special."

"Valentine's Day, you have plenty of time to plan."

I was about to say something when Odessa, standing and steadying herself on the heels, caught all my attention. She was slipping on the jacket. "She's beautiful." I didn't look away as she glanced at me and mouthed that she'd be a minute.

Abe gruffly chuckled. "You were a goner from the second you met her, weren't you?"

"Yes, and I'm not ashamed to admit that."

"You two have fun. Me and the man got the kids covered."

"Is that putting a strain on your relationship?"

"No. Lyndon's family lives in Hawaii, and he has a big family, more siblings than me so it's kinda like being at home. His family is great. Only met them through video calls, but they're not able to travel. They save up to be able to fly him home every Christmas for a few days. Last year was the first time we had a family holiday. Mom sneaked and got us or made us little things and made a small cake for our birthdays growing up. Holidays were considered a waste of resources and pagan, blah blah blah."

"I'm ready," Odessa said as she crossed the living room from her bedroom where she seemed to be placing items in my backpack.

We took the time to say bye to the kids and made our way downstairs. Her hips naturally swayed with the height of her heels, and I slowed to check out her ass in those jeans. She glanced over her shoulder, and I winked at her as she caught me.

"So, how does this work?" she asked as I removed the helmet and placed it on her head, securing the strap.

"I get on. You mount behind me and place your feet on the pegs." I pointed to where they were. "Then you hug my waist and just follow my lead. Are you nervous?"

"No, you'll always make sure I'm safe."

"I will. That's a promise I'll never intentionally break." I gave her a quick kiss, tightened the straps of the backpack, and got on.

Once I had her settled and comfortable behind me, her arms slightly tightened as the engine rumbled to life. I pulled off and headed for the city limits, then turning off onto the scenic route down the coast. Once we were on our way, I felt her gradually relax and placed her chin on my shoulder. I'd picked the perfect time and route to make it a peaceful ride. If she ended up loving it, I'd take her out more often. I loved my long rides on the weekends, just riding until I ended up wherever.

I knew she had a camping trip on her list, a tent, fire, and smores. Maybe we could make it a family trip—us, the kids, and Abe's boyfriend. I wanted to be included in their tight-knit unit and felt the need to show her they were as important as her. I smiled as she slipped her hands in the pocket of my jacket and made a mental note to pick her up a pair of gloves. It wasn't a chilly night but being so near the ocean made it cooler.

Minutes passed, and I finally saw the sign for the turnoff. I had a friend with a house on the beach just a short walk to the restaurant and a safe place to stow my bike. She'd given me the keys and garage door opener. The sensor triggered the doors, and I slowly pulled into the garage.

"This doesn't look like a restaurant," she said full of snark as I helped her off the seat and held her hand while she steadied herself.

"No, it's not. This is a friend's house. She gave me a spare key and the garage door opener to park here while we have dinner and take part in the rides and games on the boardwalk. How does that sound?" I dismounted and removed my helmet, took hers, and placed them on a workbench.

"Sounds like fun."

"I hope so. What do you need from the backpack? I can put it in my pocket."

"Just my wallet. I threw in a few things in case…"

"So I won't have to beg you to spend the night?" I asked as I approached her, slipped the straps off her shoulders, and tossed the bag to join the helmets. I palmed her hips and stroked around to the curves of her plump ass cheeks. She wrapped her arms around my neck as I leaned down until my mouth touched hers. I groaned as I teased the seam of her lips with my tongue and squeezed the lush curves in my hands. "I missed you all week," I whispered before I crushed my lips against hers as she lifted onto her toes. She arched, pressing her large breasts to my chest.

I turned us until I backed her up until her ass hit the edge of the bench, and I bent my knees to lift her onto the wooden top. Wedging my hips between her thick thighs, I roughly tangled my tongue with hers as I desperately unzipped her jacket until I could get my hands under her soft t-shirt and palm her soft, beautiful tits through the lace cups of her bra. Her nipples were hard and thick as I squeezed them between my middle and index fingers. Her breath hitched, and her lips fell lax.

"So sensitive." I stroked my lips along her cheek, down the side of her neck, sucking at her silky skin.

"Dani," she whined.

"Easy, babygirl, I know what you need." I shoved her shirt up to expose the crimson lace that cupped her breasts perfectly. I knew she wore the matching panties I'd bought her. I drew her right nipple between my teeth and bit down as I roughly tugged at the button of her jeans and eased her zipper down. "I'm going to lick that sexy pussy. You're gonna let me, right, baby?" I chuckled darkly as she fisted her fingers in my hair, and I bit down on her nipple. The large peak filled my mouth as I sucked until my cheeks hollowed.

My pussy clenched, and I felt the wetness gathering at being the one to turn her on, to make her lose control. "Lift," I ordered as I curled my hands in the sides of her waistband of denim and panties. As she obeyed, I tugged until I stripped them down to her knees. I fell to mine, and she tilted her hips as my breath fanned her fuzzy pussy. I licked my lips as I used my left hand to part her slit, flicked her clit, and played with the hood that still partially covered her little nub.

I growled at the first taste of her, her flesh wet against my chin as I dug my fingers into her outer thighs, my fingertips sunk easily into her softness. I jerked her closer to the edge. I groaned as she tried to open her legs wider, but the fabric around her knees kept her from spreading herself for me. My gaze moved up her rounded belly with the silvery marks to find her playing with her nipples. And as I gave her head, I watched her face, the way her eyes were squeezed shut. The beautiful flush of her cheeks.

The suckling sounds grew louder as she grew wetter as I tongued her tight hole, felt the flex of it, and slipped two fingers deep, stretching her open as I gently teased her clit, lapped at it, rolled my tongue over it, and suckled. I didn't set a rhythm to keep her on edge. She was whining and grunting, her hips rolling as she fucked herself onto my face and fingers.

I retreated only far enough to look at her, take in the slickness, the flush, and the way she took my middle and ring finger. "Show me how much you want me to fuck you..." Her eyes flew open, and she met my gaze. "Don't be shy, babygirl.

If we were at home, you'd be naked and bent over my bed. But this will have to do."

I knew the minute her body and desire overruled her natural shyness. She placed her hands on the bench and bounced her sexy body until her tits, belly, and thighs jiggled. I loved every movement, every shift...every dirty, little whimper that passed her lips. She grew wetter as she slammed herself down on my fingers. I couldn't take anymore, so I buried my face in her plump lips and tortured her clit, and found her sweet spot, rubbing as I licked her and loved every second of her soaking my face. She became a vice around my fingers, her strong thighs clenching around my head as she screamed, and I ate her out until she was shaking uncontrollably above me.

My name a tortured litany on her tongue as she sunk the fingers of her right hand into my hair and pulled me deeper. Soaking my face, filling my nose with her scent, and her taste permanently etched onto my tastebuds. My pussy pulsed, and my own hips were restless, but this was hers, a release just to make her feel good. I didn't stop until her body seemed to collapse, and I quickly slipped from the v of her thighs and the barrier of her pants and panties. I surged to my feet, grabbed her cheeks in my hands, and slammed my mouth onto hers—sharing the flavor of her release with her. I brought her down gently.

"Dani."

"That's going to be my favorite pastime." We both breathed heavily as she hugged me, and I soothed her with the stroke of my hands under the back of her shirt. I pressed small kisses to her lips and then rested my forehead to hers.

"I think I made a big mess."

"Nothing that won't clean up. Let me find something to help out, and then I'll take you inside to find a bathroom. I definitely need to wash my face." She blushed. "Babygirl, don't be embarrassed. You'd be naked and spread out for several rounds if we were at home." I reluctantly stepped away from her, looking around until I spotted some paper towels, grabbed a couple, and returned to tenderly clean her so she could be comfortable enough to go wash up. I helped her down, pulled up her pants, and handed her the keys to get inside. I found a bottle of cleaner to take care of the mess she'd made on the bench top. Then I went to wash my face and hands. I was determined to take her on our first date. I'd been looking forward to it all week.

I pushed aside the discomfort of my arousal and felt it ease as I made myself presentable, and I smiled as a shy Odessa appeared in the kitchen. I held out my hand, and as she took it. I got us on our way to the restaurant and held her hand the entire way there.

She kept glancing at me as her heels clicked on the side-walk and then turned hollow as we stepped onto the wooden patio that led to the front door. I'd made a later reservation so we wouldn't have to rush. The hostess asked my name, and I gave it and the time I asked for. Luckily, our table was ready, and I released Odessa's hand and motioned her to precede me. I motioned her into the booth and followed her in. We ordered drinks, and the hostess left the menus.

"What should I get?" she asked without opening her menu and laid her chin on my shoulder to look at mine.

"Depends. What do you like?"

"I'm not picky."

"Okay, I'll order for you."

"This is my first date...ever."

"Not even in high school? Some movie and popcorn, making out in a back row?"

"No." She laughed. "My parents watched me so closely that I couldn't even sneak out. I never got to do all the fun things my few friends in high school got to do. Our community was pretty small, and the friends I had that weren't...I guess I was too embarrassed to invite them over or whatever."

"Sounds lonely." I turned my head to brush my lips to hers.

"It was. What about you? You were probably popular in high school."

"I was, but I didn't have much of a social life. Sports and academics took up all my time. I was always training. My parents set aside money my entire life for a college fund, and it would've covered everything. But when I planned on a doctorate, I needed to do well enough for scholarships. I didn't want to spend the rest of my life paying off student loans. I graduated a year and a half early, got early admission, and pushed to finish my doctorate in half the time."

"You sound driven."

I was about to answer as the server appeared with our drinks, and I placed our orders for appetizers and main courses. I waited until she left to turn my full attention back to my baby.

"Probably more than I should've been. My moms kept telling me to enjoy life...have some fun because real life happened soon enough. And then, I blew out my knee, and I was thankful for the academic scholarships. Even with surgery and rehab, my knee wouldn't be good enough to go back to competing. And let me tell you, I pushed myself to the breaking point to try. What about you? What happens after school?"

"I don't know. It's just something I wanted to finish. An unofficial list, I guess. Did I thank you for the list idea?"

"No need, I'm having just as much fun as you. I thought we could go camping in the spring, maybe take the kids with us, or not." I smirked at her. "Just you and me in a tent, preferably some place isolated so I can keep you naked. Skinny dipping with you is on *my* list."

"Of course it is."

"You do know I'm picturing you in that sexy bra and panties I bought you, right? Or even better naked?" She hid her face from me. I loved the mix of confidence and shyness that was all Odessa. "Baby, look at me." I waited until she lifted her head. "You're adorable when you blush," I said quietly as I stroked the pink that highlighted her cheekbones.

"Don't. You're making it worse." She looked up at me from under her thick lashes. "I feel really good when I'm with you."

"And that's all I want. Okay, not all. I want you, every sweet, brilliant, and strong inch of you. I wasn't just saying that I wanted this to work to get something from you. Like I said, I wasn't planning what happened last weekend, but I in no way regret that it did."

"I thought it would...that it would be awkward afterward, but it wasn't."

"Just a lot of changes in a short period of time, and you need time to process. Babygirl, you have all the time you need. Until you say otherwise, I'm not going anywhere." I stroked her cheek and kissed her forehead as our food arrived. "Eat, and then we'll go have some fun."

All I wanted to do was build Odessa up until she didn't need me but chose me anyway. It showed respect for her autonomy, her fierce independence, and that's what you always did for your partners no matter what.

Chapter Eleven

ODESSA

I'd reached a surreal moment in my life. I was in the bedroom I shared with my daughter, and I stared into a mirror as all four of my children and Abe's boyfriend tried to help me pick out something to wear for Thanksgiving later that day. A dinner where I was meeting my girlfriend's parents. That was not a situation I ever saw myself in. In our community, everyone knew everyone from church and get-togethers. I'd never been introduced to the parents before.

"You're having a panic attack." Michael rolled his eyes at me.

"Do you blame me?"

"Ma, you're both adults. It's not like they're going to throw you out of the house and tell you to never see their daughter again. You're completely losing your shit right now."

"You're not helping, Abe." I glanced over my shoulder to see Lyndon leaning back against my son's chest as Lyndon gave me an encouraging smile. At least my son's boyfriend wasn't picking on me.

"Abe's right, though. You've been dating Dani for what, over two months now? And don't try the *we've only been*

dating X amount of weeks, you were dating since the diner."
Denise was a traitor.

"I thought at least my daughter would have my back on this one."

"We all do." Gabriel crawled off the bed. "We think they'll like you no matter what because you make Dani happy. It's the reason we like Dani."

My children's easy acceptance of their mother dating a woman shocked me a bit. That shouldn't have, though. They were amazing and smart, and they'd adapted easily to life outside the strictness of our former life. Yes, they still had days where the strangeness of freedom overwhelmed them a bit, but I just allowed them time to process.

"I got this. You're overthinking too much, and your kids are too nice to outright tell you to stop, but I'm not." Lyndon jumped off the bed. He was an inch taller and more muscular than my son, and he was on an academic scholarship but played college football. He passed me to look through my closet, pulling things off the hangers. "This blouse, with your hair and skin, perfect color, jeans, the faux leather jacket, and the stiletto boots. There, done." He shoved the clothes into my arms. "Appropriate but comfortable."

"Thank you."

"You're welcome. And Professor Waters is pretty chill. I took her intro class freshman year. Played basketball a few times at the courts. She's vicious when she plays. And from what Abe has told me, very fond of you." As he winked at me, I smiled. "Go get ready. It's almost time for her to pick us up. You'll ride with her, and Abe and I have the kids."

I nodded and carried the clothes to the bathroom. I liked the young man Abe chose. They'd started dating at the beginning of Abe's freshman year—almost two years—I felt a bit of sadness and regret that he hadn't felt comfortable coming to me, but as with all my kids, they had their own way of processing. I dressed, applied a bit of makeup, and again styled my hair that I'd learned from a video I'd watched for people with wavy hair. I didn't have the patience or inclination to straighten and do all that. Makeover or not, I was pretty low-maintenance and preferred it that way.

Although, I'd noticed the compliments and questions I received from my bosses and co-workers. I'd told Martin, my lawyer, about Dani and asked if that would cause issues. I'd gotten sole custody of the kids on statements made by them and Jenna about the conditions in the home and community. Jed was fighting child and spousal support and the divorce, but Martin said dating wasn't endangering my children. They were also old enough to decide where they wanted to live, and that was with me, even in the too-tiny apartment.

I cursed as a knock sounded, hurried to finish getting ready, and stepped out of the bathroom. From Dani's indulgent expression, my children had snitched me out.

"They betrayed me, didn't they?"

"Aw, babygirl." She enclosed me in her arms and cuddled me to her chest. "No need to be nervous. The moms are going to love you." She tipped my head up with her fingertips under my chin. "Beautiful as always," she whispered just before her lips brushed mine.

"We're going downstairs. We're following you and Ma to your parents' place."

Abe cleared the kids and Lyndon out not so subtly, and Dani laughed as the door closed. "Polite of them to leave me alone with you."

"They've apparently been matchmaking since Michael asked if you could come to dinner."

"I had a feeling, and I was grateful for the invitation. How long do you think we have before they're calling us?"

"Not that long."

"I wouldn't be so sure, getting you off to relax before..."

"No, behave." I bit at my bottom lip.

"You know I love it when you get nervous and do that, right?" She stroked my lower lip with the pad of her thumb. "I love everything you do, but I want you to relax. My moms are excited to meet you and the kids. They complain they haven't already. Told me I was being selfish and not sharing, and I told them they were right. All you have to do is have fun. This isn't some interview. To me, they can love you or not because nothing they say will make me stop seeing you."

"But I want them to like me," I whined.

"I guarantee they will. You have everything?"

"Just have to grab my purse and the cake I made to take." I narrowed my eyes as she opened her mouth. "It's polite to take something, and we're bringing five teenagers and a twenty-one-year-old with massive appetites."

"Fine. After you, babygirl."

I continued with my mental pep talk through grabbing my purse and the lemon cake and all the way across the city to an outlying suburb. Dani knew what I needed, so she didn't push me to talk. She'd gotten so used to me going quiet when I was thinking that she just held my hand. I could do this. No panic attack. I was strong and confident, I adored Dani, and I wouldn't mess up my first impression by having a meltdown. Please don't let me be lying to myself.

We parked in the driveway of a two-story home at the end of a cul-de-sac. It was a beautiful home with a white picket fence and everything.

"This is home?" I glanced over my shoulder to see the kids park behind Dani's vehicle.

"Yeah, this is the house I grew up in. They bought it as a fixer-upper. They'd initially thought once they finished, they'd sell it, but the moms loved it too much. That's what Mama does. She does renovations and also buys and flips houses. Mama builds-renovates them. Ma makes them pretty from the yard to inside. I swear if they were forced to work away from each other, they wouldn't survive."

Just then, a petite couple walking out of the front door drew my attention. They were both average height, one was leanly muscled, and the other was beautiful with a slim build. "Those are your moms?"

"Yep, that's the weird ones. Sit tight."

I rolled my eyes at her order. I knew not to get out on my own. As much as I gave her a hard time, I loved the way she spoiled me with love, affection, and care. It was natural for her, and I couldn't fault her for that. I smiled as Dani opened the door, leaning in to release my seatbelt. She held my hand as I slid from the seat. I cupped her cheek as she gave me three quick kisses, and I loved the feel of her smile against my lips.

"I'll get your purse and the cake."

"You're late," a femininely husky voice yelled from a short distance away.

"I had precious cargo."

"It appears you did, and more behind you."

"Odessa, meet my Ma, Freya, and my mama, Aggie. Moms, this is my girl, Odessa." She introduced me and then the kids to her moms.

"I'm so excited to meet all of you. Dani has told me so much about you and your kids. We have a houseful arriving soon, but we have a few hours of just family time." Freya motioned the kids to follow her.

Dani braced her arm across my lower back and cupped my opposite hip, giving it a gentle squeeze. "See, just normal parents, well, normal-ish. Don't tell them I called them normal."

We entered the house and walked through the foyer and down the hallways. I paused at a wall of pictures. I took in Dani from newborn through her graduations, and more recent ones that looked like family portraits.

"Ma loves pictures. The house is filled with them. Her parents didn't take many growing up, and when they cut off contact with her, she had a few that she'd been given. But basically, she lost all her memories in the guise of pictures and mementos. So she wanted to document every second."

"I know how she feels. I lost a lot of that when I left. I pretty much grabbed everything of the kids." I stared at the wall for a few more minutes and then entered the kitchen with Dani behind me.

There was a bit of pain in the center of my chest seeing Dani's parents interact with my children. It was a scene of what I assumed a happy family would look like. Even when we'd have family dinners, there wasn't a lot of laughter or conversation. I remembered the silence more than anything. A tension that grew so thick it felt as if it closed your throat.

As the hours passed, some conversations bordered on interrogations that made Dani groan, and my kids loudly laughed. I met so many people I'd never remember all their names. We ate and laughed, and as the day wound down, Dani, the kids, and I, along with her moms, went out back to sit around a fire pit. Dani pulled me down on her lap. The old me would've protested the open displays of affection, the random kisses, and touches. Yet, I'd noticed that Freya and Aggie showed each other the same affection, to the point it was just natural. Abe sat on the ground between Lyndon's legs, and Lyndon hugged Abe's neck.

I tried to imagine that scene back in Utah—tried to place my biological family and in-laws doing the same. I couldn't do that because propriety would've won out. Such obscene displays were frowned upon. Hell, even behind closed doors, there was no love. All of it was rather sad and depressing. Months ago, I'd thought of holding out until all the kids graduated, and then I'd return home to beg forgiveness. Currently,

I couldn't even stomach the thought of seeing my parents or ex again.

"Hey, why the frown?" Dani whispered close to my ear. "Are you tired? Do you want to go home?"

I shook my head and pressed my mouth to hers. "Involuntary contrast and compare happened in my head. I tried to place my family, ex-husband, and in-laws in this scenario."

"Couldn't do it?"

"No."

"Good thing you don't have to worry about that anymore. Think you can handle Christmas with us, too? Because it'll just be a repeat of today."

"I think I can handle that."

"Good, I wasn't going to give you a choice."

"You're awful bossy."

"But, babygirl, you like it when I'm bossy, and I'm going to show you just how much this weekend."

"It's a date."

She hugged me tight to her chest, and her breath teased the side of my neck. I couldn't wait until we were alone. I was more than a little addicted to sleeping in her bed and waking up with her curled around me. It was safety and comfort, and Dani was the only person who'd made me feel safe while taking some of the weight from my shoulders.

Chapter Twelve

DANI

Music blasted in my earbuds as I pushed into my fourth of my six-mile morning run. I'd slacked for several weeks as I was having a hard time sleeping at night. With the kids spending weekends with Abe or their friends, it left Friday to Sunday evening for Odessa and me. I'd grown used to sleeping with my girl in my arms, and the before-bed calls weren't enough. Four months passed since I'd met her, and three since we'd officially started dating and were about to spend our first Christmas together.

I kept trying to remind myself I needed to go at her pace. Whether people would think it was too soon, I loved her and her kids. I felt as if everything up until that point was just me biding my time until she arrived. Fate or something else, it didn't matter to me. We weren't at the moving-in stage or any of that, but I wanted it all with her. She still had the divorce to get through, and I knew she was stressed because her ex wouldn't sign the papers.

I turned the last corner headed back to my building, and my phone started ringing in my ear. I connected the call.

"Waters."

"Dani, I need you to get to Ma's. Father found out where she lived."

I picked up speed, ignoring the twinge in my knee, and slowed when I stopped by my SUV. "Abe, calm down. I'll be on my way in a few minutes. Is she alone?"

"She called the cops, but he's demanding to see the kids. I got Lyndon's car keys, but you're closer."

Fear tightened my chest at what could've happened, but I shoved those thoughts aside as I slid my keys into the ignition. "I'll take care of it. Just get there when you can."

I disconnected the call as I merged onto the empty street. It was still early enough that traffic wasn't bad. Thankfully, the kids would've already left to get to school. After the longest fifteen minutes of my life, I pulled into the alley between the two buildings as two cop cars blocked the front. I was out and running, taking the stairs was faster as the building elevator was slow as fuck.

"Odessa."

A cop stopped me. "You can't come in."

"My girlfriend is in there. Her son called me."

He turned to look over his shoulder, and he was just tall enough I couldn't look over his shoulder. "We have a..."

"Dr. Dani Waters."

"A Dr. Waters out here. She says she's the girlfriend."

"Dani!" My baby's voice broke, and I barely waited for the officer to move out of the way.

From the corner of my eye, I saw a big, angry-looking man in jeans and a dress shirt with the buttons done up to his throat, but I ignored him as Odessa reached for me.

"Hey, babygirl, it's okay." I cupped her cheeks that were soaked with tears. "Abe called me."

"He was the last person I called. I just hit redial."

"You did just fine. Are you okay? Did he..." She roughly shook her head. "Did you call Martin?"

"Yes. He's on his way to explain that I have sole custody, but he's refusing to leave without the kids." She fisted her hands in the side of my shirt, and I felt how hard they were shaking.

"He's not getting our kids. Say it."

"He's not getting our kids."

"Good girl. Come here and sit down, and I'll get you something to drink." I led her to the couch and noticed she was still wearing her gown. "Can she get dressed while I make her some coffee?"

"Sure."

"Babygirl, go change, and once you come back, I'll have your morning coffee. I know how cranky you get." I softly kissed her and noticed her trying to turn to see the bastard. "No, he doesn't exist, just you and me. Look right at me." She locked her gaze with mine. "What are you?"

"Safe."

"That's right, always safe. You're the boss here." She rolled her eyes. "For the most part. Go get dressed and wash your face." I patted her hip and dropped a kiss to the top of her head. I didn't take my focus from her until she closed the bedroom door.

I went to the kitchen to make a pot of coffee. She needed the caffeine, and I did, too. While I waited for it to brew, I sent a text to Greta to tell her I had a family emergency and to get her to cover my classes or cancel the ones she couldn't find someone to take.

"You son of a bitch." Abe's enraged voice had me running from the kitchen just as I saw the cops grab him as he went for his father.

"Abe, son, go check on your mama, please." He turned to

me with his eyes filled with pain and anger. Almost two decades of trauma rushing to the surface. "She's getting dressed. Take care of her for me."

"Okay, Dani."

The four officers watched Abe warily. His size made him a bit intimidating. I leaned my shoulder against the entryway and smirked at the bastard, taking in his pale skin mottled red at someone else taking the lead in his family. A family he'd been stupid enough to mistreat. The fact I was a woman was killing him; I could see it in the way his fists flexed at his sides.

"Dani," Martin called my name as he came through the open front door. "Is she okay?"

"She's in the bedroom with Abe."

"I'm Martin Sanchez. I'm Mrs. Grier's attorney. Mr. Grier has no order of visitation to see the minor children, and I filed for an emergency protection order."

"She's my wife, and she's coming home."

"No, Mr. Grier, you've had six months to sign the paperwork we sent to your lawyer. We've established irreconcilable differences and evidence of abuse of Mrs. Grier and her children in the almost twenty years of your farce of a marriage. And the fact you're not in cuffs concerns me." Martin sent all the officers a scathing look.

"God—"

"We're talking law, Mr. Grier, not God, because your religion has no bearing on our legal proceedings. And the fact that you terrorized my client is just another reason I'm going to ask the judge to sign off on the divorce."

We all turned as the lock on the door clicked, and it opened to expose my girl with her hair down around her shoulders, in jeans and a v-neck t-shirt that dipped to expose her cleavage. I glanced at Abe to see him grinning.

"Odessa, are you okay?" Martin asked.

"Yes, I'm sorry to call you so early."

"My husband and I were up with the kids, no problem. You know you can call me any time."

The sound of disgust from the bastard as he would forever be known caused Odessa to tense. I held out my hand, and she came right to me, cuddling against my side. She fisted her hands in my ratty t-shirt that was still a bit damp with sweat.

"You're disgusting, immoral, with this...thing."

"He's not very loquacious, is he? I'd hoped for something, hell, an old-school slur."

"Dani." She pinched my flat belly.

"Yes, dear," I whispered as I watched Abe take his place on her other side. I gripped the back of his shirt with my right hand and gave it a tug until he looked at me. I could see he was barely holding it together. The physical manifestation of his fears and shame stood just across the room. Everything Abe had done by his father's orders, playing out in his head. No matter his mother telling him to obey, that it was okay, it would never fully alleviate the guilt.

"I'm okay. No, I'm not, but I will be."

"I want you to text the kids, tell them you're picking them up after school, and you're all staying at my place tonight. Just to be safe."

"I got it covered. Can Lyndon stay, too?"

"Of course."

"Thanks."

"No need."

Just as Martin was talking to the cops, an elderly couple walked in, who had to be Odessa's parents. While my girl was softer and lighter, her mother was stiff with a look of eternal judgment on her face.

"Why haven't my grandchildren been returned to us yet?" The elderly man asked.

"Why would you think you were going to get the children?" Martin asked.

"She's unfit to care..."

"You're not taking my children from me," Odessa yelled.

"She's very right. The minor children have been assessed by a court-appointed psychologist. We have glowing reports from child services, and the minor children are all fifteen and older, which means they are cognizant enough to determine where they want to live. They have emphatically declared their wishes to stay with their mother. With the refusal to pay child support or support of any kind, Mrs. Grier has been issued sole custody, and any visitation is at her discretion, which I'm sure her and her partner will agree, you're not getting."

"Abe, you will retrieve your siblings and bring them home," Odessa's father demanded.

"No, not happening. My boyfriend and I are picking them up and going to Dani's, and that's the only place we're going. Your pastor might run that community, but it doesn't mean shit here."

The shock on their faces would've been almost comical if the hate wasn't thick enough to choke everyone in the room. What was right in front of me showed me in glaring detail what Odessa and her kids experienced. The boys would've grown into angry and resentful men, Denise would've been broken by living to some archaic standard of what the expectations were for a godly young woman. I was painfully aware of what insular communities could do to their members. I was horrified at what would've happened if my girl hadn't made her escape.

"Abe, go pack an overnight bag for the boys while we do one for Denise, and I'll give you the key to the apartment. Your mama has a spare for when we're done here."

"You're not in charge of my family," the bastard bellowed.

"No, I'm not. Odessa is, and as her partner, it's my duty to support her and her wishes. And for her safety, until I know you're back to your hateful little community, her and the kids will be safe with me."

"It's a woman's place to obey." Her father pointed a bony finger in my direction.

I laughed and reveled in their shock. "No, it's not. She and Denise will never obey to protect the status quo. That's not how it works. I adore your daughter, and her decision to get a divorce and be happy is paramount. Nothing is more important than that to me." I felt the stares but none more powerful than Odessa tipping her head back to stare at me. "Martin, I think it's time for them to leave, and if they don't..."

"I'll take care of it."

"Come on, babygirl, let's go pack you and Denise bags." I shifted and placed my hands on her waist, and I led her to the room she shared with her daughter, kicking the door closed behind us.

As soon as we were locked in, she turned and threw herself against my chest. She sobbed as if her heart were breaking, and maybe it was. This was the first time in almost two years she'd seen her ex and her parents, and they demeaned everything she'd worked for.

"Hey, you know what happens when you're sad?" I took her face in my hands and lifted her face away from my chest. "There shouldn't ever be sadness in those gorgeous eyes or on this adorable face." She hiccupped a laugh. When I called her adorable, it was a fix every time.

"I got too comfortable."

"Odessa, you didn't get too comfortable. You found your safety and happiness for your kids. There is nothing wrong with that. You've spent over a year relearning who you are and what you want and deserve in life. There's nothing ungodly or shameful about any of that. You confronted your fears, made a conscious effort to deal with your trauma...found some pretty substantial self-confidence. *You* should be extremely proud of that."

"What about you? Are you proud..."

"I brag about you to anyone who listens. Ask Greta. I think she's getting sick of me showing off my woman and her amazing kids."

"I can see that."

"Odessa, those people in the living room, the ones who decided that they could bully you by coming here? They didn't expect a fight. They thought you'd immediately cave."

"But I had to call for help. I couldn't do it by myself."

"Help isn't a bad thing. The bastard quite literally tried to break you. Your fight-or-flight response kicked in, and even when you called for help, you still stood strong."

"I just...I want it to end. I want to be able to have my dates with you and us and the kids hanging out. What if they'd come when the kids were alone?"

"But that's not what happened, and I think Gabe and Mike would've fought hard for themselves and Denise. And she does have a killer jab."

Odessa giggled. "She does, doesn't she?"

"Let's pack while Martin takes care of the mess out there."

"Oh shit, you have to call Greta. You're going to be late."

"Already sent her a text. She's going to cover what classes she can...see if someone can take over my higher-level classes or cancel them. Greta has one lecture this afternoon, so she should just have to cancel the one."

"Okay, she hates the freshman class."

"She does. It'll pay her back for giving me shit."

We ignored the yelling on the other side of the door as I kept her distracted from the chaos. No one else existed in that apartment except for us.

"Dani?" I saw the sadness shift in her eyes to something else.

"Yeah?"

"Did you mean what you said out there?"

"Of course, you know I don't say anything to you I don't mean. You and your kids are the best thing to happen to me in years, and I adore all five of you. Yeah, we're going to have rough times, and we're going to fight. It's my belief that happy and healthy couples fight on occasion, and there's always the make-up sex. I think that's the best part."

"Of course you'd think that. Maybe one day we can test that theory."

"I'll think of ways to piss you off." I kissed her as I whispered the words against her lips, and again, I loved the feel of her smile...that I'd put it there.

We separated as she went through Denise's small dresser, and I packed my girl a bag for a few days. Abe or I would come back if they needed more or we forgot something. Unfortunately, they hadn't cleared the room yet when we exited. Abe stood toe-to-toe with his father.

"Stay here." I dropped her bag and rushed across the room. "Abe, he's not worth it. None of them are. Hitting him only hurts you...no matter how good it'll feel."

"You're a whore." Abe and I spun at the same time just in time to see her father nearly strike Odessa. She grabbed his wrist and countered the motion at the same time. "You will be judged."

As much as I wanted to jump in, this was my girl's show. The moment where she needed to stand up and finally say enough was enough. I'd gotten her and the kids in self-defense training, just in case.

"You can call me what you want, nothing I haven't heard a thousand times from you, him," She nodded her head toward the bastard. "Her...the entire community. I heard everything, and I obeyed as I was trained to do. But I'm not doing it anymore. If my children marry, it'll be for love, and if they don't, that's fine, too. They won't be forced to have children because the bible claims they must be fruitful. They're going to understand that love and existence doesn't require submission or feeling or inflicting pain. I don't want any of you here. Martin?" She released her father's wrist and stepped back as the cops converged and got her parents and ex-husband out of the apartment.

"Odessa, I hate to cause any more stress, but until I find out what their plan was in coming here, I don't want you in this apartment alone," Martin said.

"Dani said we could stay with her for a few days."

"Stay as long as you want." She could stay forever if she wanted.

"I'm going to call and check on the protective order and see if it's made it in front of a judge yet. You take the day off to get settled in at Dani's, and just let me know if you want to take another personal day for a long weekend."

"Thanks, Martin."

"Honey, when you came to me and told me about what was going on, there was no way I wasn't going to help. I know it sucks to be patient, but you're doing everything right. I asked for a copy of the police report, and if I could get statements from Dani and Abe for the file, that'd be great, too."

"Whatever you need," I said as I removed my house key from the ring and handed it to Abe. He'd come by a few times, so he knew where to go. "Just let me know when. I think Odessa just needs to go somewhere quiet and relax for a bit." We all said goodbye until I was left alone with Odessa. "How are you feeling?"

"Tired, but okay. I was always waiting for them to show up, ya know? It was kinda...anticlimactic."

"I was looking for more fire and brimstone. Let's go home. You can relax and take part in daytime television, or since we have an entire day before our chaperones arrive, maybe I could interest you in more sweaty entertainment."

"I don't think much persuasion would be needed." She draped her arms over my shoulders.

"You're so easy, and I love that about you." I grabbed her bag from the floor and dragged her toward the door with her giggling behind me.

Chapter Thirteen

ODESSA

I smoothed the crimson silk over the prominent curve of my belly and then adjusted the sides of my matching thong. I took in my reflection, catching my smile, and wondered if I'd ever get used to how my new life felt. How had I lived without the confidence I'd gained in such a short time?

As much as I loved spending time with Dani and the kids, her apartment had been crowded, and we were back to me at her place on the weekends. The kids at Lyndon's apartment with Abe. I'd felt a bit awkward about doing more than sleeping with Dani with the kids close by. I'd discovered I wasn't particularly quiet.

I fluffed my waves, gave myself one last once over, and turned off the light as I opened the bathroom door. It was nice having two bathrooms and not fighting over one. Which there was a lot of fighting with four people. As I stepped into the bedroom, the lights were dimmed, and the bed was turned down. Dani was nowhere to be seen, and just as I was about to call her name, she snuck up behind me.

My stomach tightened as she nuzzled the side of my neck. I arched my hips as her left hand teased the small triangle of silk of my panties. I lifted my right arm to reach back to hug her neck. No matter how innocent or light the touch, she had the power to make me need.

I'd learned I was completely obsessed with sex with Dani.

"Now, now, is my babygirl trying to tease me?" she asked, and I turned in her arms.

"Is it not working?"

"You just have to whisper my name, and I want you. When did you buy this? I wasn't there." She slipped her fingers under the thin straps of the teddy that barely contained the mass of my breasts and exposed the upper edge of my dark nipples.

"I took a long lunch the other day. I have a lot more."

"And to think you didn't like shopping, now, look at you. Buying sexy things on your lunch break."

"Just for you." I placed my hands on her sides and stroked lower until I reached the hem of her tank top and slipped my hands beneath the soft cotton. I counted the subtle ridges of her abs and felt her skin prickle with goosebumps

Her small breasts just filled my hands. "Take it off, please?" I asked as I watched her from under my lashes, and she grabbed the cotton and tore it over her head. I leaned in and wrapped my lips around her hard, pointed nipple and sucked.

"I'll let you have your fun, but you tease me too much... you'll take your punishment and like it." Her voice was gruff as she fisted her hands in my hair, the tug stinging my scalp.

Her skin turned slick under my hands as I licked my way down the center of her belly. As I fell to my knees, I tugged her boxer briefs down her legs. I nuzzled the thin strip of hair and inhaled her scent. I naturally submitted to her dominance, and I loved being under her control. Eating her out had become my favorite thing.

"My baby loves giving her woman head."

"I do." I kissed right at the top of her slit. I hardened my tongue and pushed until I worked her clit with just the tip. My panties grew uncomfortably slick as I parted her pussy lips with my fingers and gently kissed the hard nub. I whimpered.

"That s right, be a good girl and suck it."

I shifted my hips as she called me a good girl, and I buried my face between her thighs. I started to move my free hand between my legs.

"No, that's mine. I'm going to strap up and fuck that tight pussy." She combed her fingers through my hair. "You want that, don't you, babygirl?"

I just nodded as I suckled and pulled back until her clit almost slipped from between my lips.

"Goddamn, baby." She hissed as I ate her pussy loudly and messy, just the way I knew she liked. "Going to spank that pretty, dimpled ass as I fuck that tight cunt." Her lower abs tightened, and she shook. She was so wet and hot. She shifted until she lifted her left leg over my shoulder, pulling my head deeper. "Gonna make my good girl scream." My free hand came up, and I pushed two fingers into her, and she cursed loudly as her muscles spasmed. "Get your fucking ass up and bend over the bed." The grit in her tone made my chest tighten, and I reluctantly released her clit and slipped my fingers free. Her thigh slipped off my shoulder.

I got to my feet, and she grabbed my chin roughly and slammed her mouth down on mine. Her tongue forced its way past my lips, and I started trembling from head to toe.

"Strip. You know how much I love seeing my good girl naked."

I took a few steps backward as I removed the teddy, watched her as she licked her lips as she took in every roll, the lushness of my belly and my plump pussy as I pushed the silk of my panties off to slide down my big thighs.

"Every inch of you, not enough time to love you the way you deserve, but I'm going to make sure you are well-fucked before the night is over. Now, bend over the bed."

I swallowed hard as I obeyed, bent at the waist, and braced my hands on the soft mattress. My breasts were heavy and swayed with my quickened breaths. I loved the anticipation, the way she made me wait, and need and nervousness collided. She'd used her fingers and vibrators but never fucked me with her toys. She'd made me pick out two dildos one day at a sex shop, along with other things I'd found interesting, and I'd waited for the moment she'd slip on her harness.

I sensed her warmth before her hands cupped the fleshy cheeks of my ass. She spread them wide, and my arms gave out as she licked over my back hole. "I'm going to fuck that one day, too, but tonight, this is all mine." She tongued my pussy hole and then lowered to my clit. "Have you been a good girl?"

"Yes, Da—" The hard smack of her hand on my cheek cut off her name, and I twisted my fingers in the comforter.

Not once did I feel shame or insecurity as my body jiggled with the repeated strikes of her hands on one cheek and the other, over and over until my skin grew hot and tight. I pushed back and rode her tongue. She hummed as she noisily gave me head. Each time was more intense than the last. It was always better.

"Dani, I'm gonna—" I screamed in frustration as she instantly stopped, and then I felt the long thin dildo riding the crease of my ass.

I grunted as she placed her hand in the center of my back and pushed my upper body down. The soft fabric not giving my nipples enough stimulation. I felt the loss of her heat as she shifted back. She placed the tip to my soaked cunt, flexing her hips, and didn't stop until she bottomed out. I fisted my hair in both hands as she retreated and thrust, arched, and rotated her hips, fucking every squeaking grunt from me.

I lifted onto my toes and arched my hips as she kept hitting my g-spot, torturing it as I begged and screamed. My face was hot and flushed as I listened to our skin slap together as she fucked me hard and fast. My back arched upward as the intensity of the pleasure and pressure increased.

"You like taking my cock, don't you? My good girl gets all slutty."

I lifted my head as she blanketed my back and turned to take in the red highlighting her cheekbones, the way her hair stuck to her sweaty face.

"Tell me you love being fucked." She grunted against my mouth.

"I love when you fuck me." I barely got the words out as she shoved her hands under me and painfully played with my over-sensitive nipples.

"You're gonna soak my cock." She shoved her tongue past my lips as she increased her pace, taking me with hard, shallow thrusts. I squeaked as she suddenly stopped and shoved me onto the bed. "On your side." She rolled to my side, and she straddled my left leg, held the right one against her stomach as she thrust inside, and the pain made me fight her. "You can take it, so fucking hungry for it." She was in a position where I could rub my pussy against her inner thigh.

I froze as that tightening feeling grew in my belly. My mouth fell open as she hammered into me until her hips lost rhythm as she was grinding against me, and I grabbed her bicep. My nails dug into her skin as I bore down. The pressure built in my face, and a scream passed my lips as I came hard, soaking the both of us with my release.

I twisted until I fell to my back, and she came down on top of me. I took in the tortured look on her face as she rode out her own orgasm, and then she rolled off me. I pouted at her leaving me empty.

"Shit, we might need to get you a gag because I'm going to want to do that a lot," she whispered breathlessly, and I softly chuckled as I hid my face against her sweaty chest. She lovingly stroked her fingertips up and down my side.

"I won't complain." I pulled away to get on my knees, grabbed the base of the dildo, and climbed on. I whimpered as I slid all the way down. "Something about you calling me your good girl." I didn't know why but I needed more. I spread my hands over her upper abs, lifted my hips, and slid back down slowly.

"Take what you need. Good girls get rewards." She grabbed my wrists and sat up. She pinned them at the small of my back, and her mouth almost touched mine. "But, babygirl, remember this, you're only *my* good girl. I'm the only one who gets to love on and fuck you. Odessa, you're mine, and I'm going to make sure you always want to stay mine."

Tears burned my eyes, and I closed them to hide them, hoping she wouldn't notice. I wanted her to keep me but was it too soon to say so?

Chapter Fourteen

DANI

Usually, my weekends were dedicated to Odessa, but there I was with my newly acquired five kids Christmas shopping. I'd already set up Odessa's big present, she wanted a tattoo, and I'd scheduled an appointment with the best artist in the state. He had a six-month waitlist, but Greta knew him and helped me get an earlier appointment.

No, I didn't mind taking them shopping. Lyndon was my backup because I had late teens who'd never gone Christmas shopping in their lives. Lyndon had told me Abe had become overwhelmed during their first holiday together. They'd all saved up money to get Odessa and each other presents, and it was a week until the big day. The stores were packed, so online would've been better, but I wanted them to have that experience.

As we walked down a street filled with funky shops, thrift stores, and craft places, Denise slowed down until she walked beside me.

"I don't know what to get Ma." I threw my arm around her shoulders.

"This might sound like total bullshit, but she'll like anything you get her."

"I want it to be good. She got us like something little our first year free, but she didn't get anything. We didn't really understand all of this."

It broke me a bit as they talked about their life as first and second year free. Greta was already planning a freedom party when the divorce became final. That had made Odessa laugh and shake her head. She was in for a surprise when she realized Greta wasn't joking.

"What does your mama love?"

"Us...you." I saw her quick glance, and then she pretended to check out the window displays.

I felt like she wanted to talk about something. "Did that make you uncomfortable to say?"

"No. I mean, I grew up wearing skirts or dresses, hair always up...knowing I was going to get married no less than a month after I graduated. And I was going to have babies and take care of the house, be of service to..." She huffed.

"That's not your life now."

"I know, but Ma is so different...good different. Everything is strange. Abe's got a boyfriend, Ma's dating you, and it's like all the rules changed."

"Do you know what I told your mother when she explained what her life was like?" She shook her head. "I told her to be selfish. It's okay to grow up, meet someone, get married, and have kids. There's also nothing wrong with delaying it all to find yourself. To never get married. To never reproduce. It's okay to love someone no matter their gender or race. One day in the future, you're going to meet someone that changes everything for you with nothing more than their presence."

"Is that what it was like when you met Ma?"

I smiled at the memory of the diner. "I wasn't even planning to stop at the diner that night, but I didn't want to go home to an empty apartment. Heat up a frozen dinner, grab a beer, become that single professional stereotype." She giggled, and I hugged her to my side. "On my way home, there was that diner, and I pulled over. There was this adorable woman sitting in a booth. I spotted her through the window. She was so distracted she didn't notice there were still tables to sit at and agreed to let me sit with her. I gave her my number at the end of our talk and really wanted her to call."

"She mentioned she met someone who helped with her homework when she came home that night."

"I love your mother. I even adore all four of you. But that's between us. I haven't told her yet."

"Why not?"

"It's complicated."

"Isn't everything complicated in some way?"

"God, I forget how smart all four of you are. What did you learn from your parents' marriage?"

"That love is conditional even God's."

"We're not going to get into the perversion of religion by fundamentalism. That's your bridge to cross when you're ready. Growing up, my moms were obsessively in love with each other. Ma lost her biological family for loving another woman. Even through that pain, Mama loved big enough to make up for the hole that was left. So, when I realized I was a lesbian, I went into the world with the example of my parents. This beautiful and unbreakable connection, and I applied my experience of relationships from my parents to my own. And do you know what that got me?"

"Since you were single in your thirties, couldn't have been good."

Sometimes Denise made me forget she was only fifteen. All the kids seemed older than their years. While that was a good thing, it was also sad that they'd never experienced a childhood. "Vicious, little thing."

"Ma says my selective empathy is scary but adorable."

"She would." We stopped outside a store that the boys had disappeared into. "But what it got me was hurt and disillusioned. I didn't think the person for me existed."

"Until Ma?"

"Exactly. Your life is your own, honey. No one can define it except you. Not your father or your grandparents, not even your mom. You have to be selfish, willing to say no...to do shit that scares you."

"Ma wonders what life would've been like if she'd left sooner or actually went to college, but she wouldn't have us, and she said she couldn't deal with that. But she's so happy now. She didn't even smile before we left Utah...not real ones anyway."

"But which version of her do you love?"

"This one. She comes home happy. She loves working and going to school. Her weekends with you and your dates. It's just a lot, and it seems my brothers are doing so much better at all this than I am."

"You had different expectations on you. You were told your only purpose was as a wife and mother. You knew college wasn't going to be allowed. You were going to probably marry some boring guy and spend the rest of your life waiting on him hand and foot."

"Sounded horrible. I felt guilty that I didn't want to do my *duty*."

"Sucks being a girl sometimes."

"It does." A long-suffering, teenage-sized huff made me snort. "Thanks for, you know, the talk."

"I'm always here. You know where to find me."

"Not far from Ma, there's rarely space."

"Don't give me shit for wanting to cuddle my woman. Mother or not, she's very cuddly."

"Everyone within sight of you two thinks you're super-glued together."

"My love language is giving praise and affection. Building my person up. Nothing more powerful in life than being loved by a confident and self-aware woman."

"You're weird."

"Not the first time I've heard that. So are we going to get to this shopping? I got my woman her big present already, but I need to get some stuff she can open on Christmas day. If you don't find anything, we can go online and look. We'll have it delivered to my place."

"Thanks, Dani."

"You're welcome." I turned my head as I heard a knock on the glass and found Gabe motioning us inside. "Seems they may have found something. Let's go."

I released her and opened the door, and bells sounded as they softly hit the glass. She rushed forward to find her brothers, and I roamed the aisles of the eclectic antique store. Scanning the shelves until I reached the back, a glass case of jewelry drew my attention.

"See anything you want to look at?" An elderly lady with silver braids hanging over each shoulder smiled up at me.

"I need to get a spectacular present for my girlfriend."

"First Christmas?"

"Yes. Her kids and I are group shopping for her."

"Jewelry is usually a safe option."

"You don't know my Odessa. I buy her presents all the time, and she's finally stopped fussing at me for spoiling her."

"It's a person's prerogative to spoil their partner."

"My thoughts exactly," I said as the lady chuckled and I scanned the contents of the case. There was a delicate chain with a single flower pendant with a matching ring, the band looking like ivy with random placements of ruby flowers. "What's the story on that one?"

"You have good taste." She named off the stats, and it was just Odessa's size, but then she smiled. "Don't know how much of the story is true, but a young woman came in twenty years ago, said the love of her life bought them for her. He was a first responder...firefighter, I think. He didn't make it home from work. She had to pay a bill, and she sold the pieces to my mother. She refused to sell them but left them in the case because the young woman came back every week to put them on one more time. My mother tried to give them back, free, but pride can be a curse sometimes. She kept saying that if they were still there when she had the money, she'd buy them back. One week the lady didn't return...months, and then years passed. My mother had a strict policy, only sell these two pieces to someone who was truly in love."

"Are you saying I should buy them?"

"That's up to you. I'm not your lady's mother to ask your intentions."

"Her nineteen-year-old son already did that. I'll take both. Red is my baby's favorite color."

"Is it, or she just knows you like her in red?"

"Probably a bit of both." I felt as if I were being watched, and I turned my head to find the kids watching me. "Did you find something for Odessa?"

"Yes, but we need you to leave so we can buy yours. Out." Mike started shooing me from the store.

"It's like I'm already the stepparent. They have no respect for me." I paid for the necklace and ring and took the small bag she held out to me.

"Good luck." She winked at me.

I rolled my eyes as Denise started pushing me toward the front. "There's a vintage store two buildings down. That's where I'll be."

"Yes, Mama."

I didn't turn back around so they wouldn't see my smile at the talking in unison or what that simple word meant to me. I'd always wanted kids and someone my own, and I got them in the beautiful package that was Odessa and her children.

As soon as I stepped outside, I pulled out my phone and called my mama, and she answered before the second ring finished. "Hey, I thought you were out with our new grands?"

"They kicked me out of the store. I need a favor?"

"For you, name it."

"I need a house." The silence drew out, and I knew I'd shocked her. I never planned on doing more than apartment living since I was single, and suddenly I told my mama I needed an entire house.

"I got a five-bedroom, three-bath house, with an attached garage with an apartment above. It'll probably be finished in two months. The previous owners turned it into some modern hellscape. I'm remodeling for a family home."

That was a larger project than my parents normally took on. They preferred smaller remodels with a quicker turn-around. "When did you buy the modern hellscape?"

"Um, three months ago."

I laughed loudly and drew the attention of people about me. "You were being ambitious."

"Well, your ma and I were thinking positive. If you didn't need it, then we could flip like we always do."

"Do you think she'll—" My mama's snort cut me off.

"If she hasn't said she loves you yet, it's not because she doesn't. And you can use the excuse you haven't known each other long, but that's all it is...an excuse. I saw you were already a goner when you told us about her. Go with your gut, and nothing will go wrong. We'll set up a time for you to look at the house after New Years."

"Thanks, Mama."

"That woman and her kids make you happy. Fate sent you exactly what you craved when you were ready for it."

"I hope she feels the same way when I throw all these questions at her."

"She'll say yes to whatever. She's as obsessed with you as you are with her. About time I got to give you shit as payback for all the years you gave me and my woman shit. Get off the phone, spend time with our grands, and we'll get everything worked out."

I told her I loved her and disconnected the call after she reminded me that our presence was demanded on Christmas day. My brain went into instant planning mode. I wanted it all perfect, but first, I had to make sure everything worked out. I wanted everything just right for Odessa. She deserved everything.

Chapter Fifteen

ODESSA

I'd heard so many people complain about getting older, especially women, but I looked forward to forty. Especially when I got to spend it with Dani. She'd said she had something special planned. A few hours after I'd arrived at work, a huge bouquet of wildflowers arrived, almost identical to the one she brought me when she came to dinner that first time. Everyone stopped by the desk to make a comment, and Martin just winked at me whenever he passed by.

Valentine's wasn't something I celebrated. In primary school, I'd gotten cards and made crafts to take home. Outside school, I didn't have any experience with holidays, birthdays, or anniversaries. Three boxes came just after lunch with a note specifically telling me to open them alone when I got home. The black boxes with the large red ribbons taunted me until it was time to leave, and the text I sent her to let her know I was headed home earned the reply of what time to be ready. I had a surprise for her, too. The judge had signed the final papers and ordered support to be paid for my three youngest until they graduated.

I stood in my living room for ten minutes until the time

for pickup, and the kids were walking around me. The red dress had spaghetti straps and exposed my entire back, which meant no bra. The hem was asymmetrical—the longest side touched my calf, and the shortest one barely reached my knees. G-string and garter belt were in matching shades, and the lightly tan thigh-high stockings felt odd against my skin. The strappy stilettos made me glad I'd gotten used to heels.

"Where's Dani taking you?" Denise asked as she gave me a bratty grin.

"She said it was a surprise and just told me what time to be ready." I played with the tiny pendant at the base of my throat that Dani had given me for Christmas, along with the ring that I'd placed on my left hand. It felt comfortable there.

My kids had a few small presents and a cake they'd made ready when I got home from work. They'd skipped making dinner since I was going out and told me they'd grab something later.

As soon as I heard the knock, I crossed the room and opened the door to find Dani in a perfectly tailored suit with a tie that matched my dress.

"Babygirl, I knew that dress would be perfect on you." She took one step inside the door, and her arms circled my waist. "Happy birthday. You ready?"

"Yes. Are you going to tell me where we're going?"

"Absolutely not. I told you it was a surprise." She leaned down until her lips brushed my ear. "The rest of your present is at my place for later. Kids, you ready?" she asked, and I spun to see my kids running from the room.

"What's going on?"

"Well, first portion of the night is a nice family dinner. Then we'll bring them home, and then the rest of the date is a couple's night. Abe and Lyndon are meeting us at the restaurant."

"Dani."

"I know that tone, but the kids should get to celebrate your birthday with us. I even made sure they'd be presentable." She winked at me and backed me up with her arm still around my waist. "You get more beautiful every day. It's almost unfair," she whispered as she stroked her fingertips along the indent of my spine.

People talked about being addicted to things. I'd never understood that until I met Dani. I craved her affection, and she gave it so freely, almost without thought, and I didn't know how I'd lived without it before her. I truly felt confident and strong. I wouldn't say I didn't have my bad days. I walked taller, my chin up, and it was as if I could take on anything.

"What're you thinking about?"

"I love when you touch me too much."

"When it comes to showing you affection, it's never too much. Touch develops intimacy in all relationships platonic and romantic."

I laughed as I heard curses from the two bedrooms, and ten minutes later, my children walked out, Gabe and Mike in suits similar to Dani's, and Denise walked out in a modest black pantsuit with short heels. Her hair was twisted into a loose bun with curls framing her face. They looked so grown up.

"My babies are grown." I pouted as they groaned, and Dani laughed.

"That's what happens when you have teenagers. Okay, limo is waiting. Let's get going."

My kids rushed out of the door. "You know you're going to spoil them."

"Um, I spoil you, too."

"Thanks."

"They said they made you a cake and got you a few presents They work so hard I thought they deserved to spend at least part of the evening with us. They're amazing kids and have a lot to make up for, just like you did. Now, we gotta go before our heathens break into the mini-bar."

"That would make them your heathens and not mine."

"When they're bad, they're mine now? Is that how it's going to work?"

"Yes," I answered as she locked and closed the door behind us. "It's my birthday. I make the rules."

"Yes, dear."

I couldn't help smiling all the way down the elevator and into the limo where the kids waited. The entire night seemed strange, but I'd come to learn I liked the oddity of my new life. Where I'd spent thirty-eight years believing myself to be broken and unlovable—all it took was one terrifying step of driving across the country to a place I knew no one except one friend and my children. I built an entire life for myself outside the community. A life that I was told would lead me to ruin, and that's in no way what happened. I'd found love and a community that was open and accepting, and it started with a leap of faith.

I rested against Dani's side as she hugged me with her arm braced across my upper chest. We pulled up in front of one of the fanciest restaurants in the city. I'd made reservations for business dinners there several times. Dani kissed my shoulder and then nipped at my skin in warning. She knew I was about to protest. I'd always lived with the bare minimum. I'd learned to be frugal, and it was a hard habit to break even for her.

Abe and Lyndon were both waiting to give me a hug when I got out of the limo. Dani took my hand as she walked me into the restaurant with our brood behind us. She told the hostess the name for the reservation, and we were led to a private room in the back.

It was the best night, even when my kids sang horren-dously off-key and probably irritated most of the other customers, but we ate and laughed, and it was perfect. It couldn't get better than me with Dani and my kids.

———

"You're not tired, are you? I still have plans for us," Dani whispered in my ear several minutes after we'd dropped everyone else off at home. Abe and Lyndon were spending the night in case I was late. Even though I knew my ex-husband was back in Utah, him showing up still made me fearful of leaving my babies alone.

"No, just enjoying the quiet and hoping my ears will stop ringing from the singing."

"I thought that older couple were going to call the cops." Her laugh was muffled against the side of my neck, and then I moaned as she sucked at that spot just behind my ear.

"Are you going to tell me where we're going next?"

"We're almost there. You just have to wait another twenty minutes."

"Your apartment is in the other direction."

"Relax and let your woman have her moment."

"Fine, I have a surprise for you."

"And what is that?"

"Martin gave me a birthday present today."

"Hopefully, it was final divorce papers."

"It was."

"Congratulations. I'll have to let Greta know. She's been planning your freedom party for months."

I turned to stare at her in shock. "I thought she was joking."

"No, this is Carnegie Hall level planning. This production will put all others to shame. I did talk her out of the strippers, though, so you owe me for that one."

"That was probably more for you than me. You do *not* like to share."

She paused as if thinking it over. "True, very true. I freely admit my obsession."

"Thank you for tonight."

"You're welcome. We'll have to make the split date part of our birthday slash Valentine's Day tradition."

I loved how easily she spoke of the future and traditions. She'd always helped me find things outside of what I'd lived for decades. Replacing the bad with the good.

"I'd like that." She pinched my chin and brushed her lips to mine. This one wasn't innocent...it was a seduction.

"Fuck, we have to be good, just a little longer." Even as she said we had to be good, her kiss turned rough, and she pushed her fingers between my knees. As she stroked upward, I didn't hesitate to spread them. My lips parted as she moved the crotch of my panties aside, and my breath hitched as she rubbed my plump pussy lips, slipping between them to tease my clit. "I think I created a monster." Then she hissed against my lips.

We barely registered the car coming to a stop before we both worked to fix my panties and dress to look semi-presentable. The driver opened the back door, and Dani got out, reaching in her hand for mine. She helped me to my feet.

"You two have a great night," the driver said as he walked around to the driver's side, and a few minutes later, he was pulling away.

"Where are we?" I looked around the neighborhood. They were all large family homes, white picket fences, and perfect lawns.

"Come on. This is the final part of your surprise."

When we walked hand in hand to the front door, I noticed her vehicle parked in the driveway. Several steps led up onto a beautiful porch with rocking chairs and a swing. Baskets of flowers and plants hung from the eaves. And as I was taking it all in, she let go of my hand. She pulled out keys and unlocked the door.

"After you, babygirl." She motioned me in with a bow and a wink. I entered, and it was gorgeous inside. "Did your moms do the work?"

"Yes, this was their newest flip. I bought it."

I spun on my toes as she leaned back against the door, and then she turned the deadbolt. "You bought a house?"

"Yeah, I figured it was time." She paused to take a breath as if she braced herself for something. "I've loved you since the first shy smile you gave me."

I tensed as she pushed away from the door and slowly closed the distance between us.

"You were perfect in every way, and over the months, you just got so much...I got to witness you become confident and independent. I got to see you become a badass. I love you and your, hopefully, our kids more than anything. I want to live in this big house with you. There's room for everyone."

"Dani." My heart started beating a frantic rhythm in my chest as I took in her half-smile, and I finally realized what that look in her eyes was when she was with me. I'd never been in love, or if I ever did, that the person would return the feeling.

"I know you're not going to say it's too soon or any of that, but I just want to finish because I've been planning this since Christmas. One day I want us to get married, not tomorrow or anything, but just when you're ready. I want this to be our home, you and me, fresh start. No bad memories. Just you and me growing old and having lots and lots of sex."

I snorted even as tears rolled down my cheeks. "You do make a compelling argument, Dr. Waters."

"I thought so." She finally got close enough to circle my waist and linked her fingers at the small of my back. "What do you say? I already asked your kids' permission, even Lyndon. He was a little shocked I included him."

"Yes, I was a mess when I escaped. I threw up across several states. I swore I wasn't going to make it...wasn't going to be able to give the kids what they needed. And then I got a job, enrolled in school, and we were making it. It wasn't all perfect, but I had my kids. And when I left, that's all I wanted. Then this really gorgeous woman asked to share my table."

"Gorgeous...I'm liking this story."

I rolled my eyes at her, and she dropped a kiss on the end of my nose. "And the longer I was around you, I realized I *had* changed. Being independent made me feel strong, and then I had the newly acquired feelings for you. I want you. I want this house. I need all of it. I love you. Probably longer than I realized, but it all felt right. And I would've moved into your equally small apartment just because you were in it."

Her mouth crashed down onto mine, and I barely registered us moving. "We're going to our bedroom. We have an entire house to christen before we have to be responsible parents and keep it behind closed doors."

She spun me around and smacked my ass to get me running up the stairs. We loved each other, and I was finally going to have a home filled with love and laughter, and it would be perfect even when it wasn't.

Epilogue

DANI

Twenty Years Later

We ended every Valentine's Day the same way, her naked and riding my strap-on as I tortured her until she soaked my thighs as she came. She was sweaty and relaxed, straddling my thighs and her head resting on my chest. I played with the sides of her breasts that bulged outward where they were flattened against my belly. Twenty years, one baby added to the four we already had, sons-in-law and daughters-in-law, a bunch of grandkids, and I loved her more every year. Every gray hair, new dimples, a few more pounds or a few less, and we hadn't spent a day apart in all that time.

"Not bad for a sixty-year-old and a fifty-two-year-old. Ready for round four?"

"Let me recover from three. My ass is going to be bruised tomorrow."

"You always said you liked the reminders. Should I stop?"

Her head jerked up. "Don't you dare," she said as she

glared at me, and I grabbed her and flipped her onto her back, and then I removed the harness and dropped it over the side of the bed to rest on a towel.

I turned on my side and rested my head in my upraised hand, and took in my wife naked and satisfied. Our kids knew to call before coming over since our youngest moved out six months ago for college. We'd enjoyed our empty nest.

I wasn't as toned, even though I still ran every day. My knee was closer to needing to be replaced, but we'd aged together. Raised a beautiful family that still called our house home. They came over every Sunday for dinner. I was an old sap because I had every Mother's Day card they'd ever given me in twenty years. I walked my oldest sons and daughter down the aisle. My daughter meeting Greta at the end of the aisle, I could've done without, but Denise had weird taste.

"What are you thinking about?" she asked as I stroked her side with the backs of my fingers.

"Twenty years of being yours."

"I still think I got the better deal."

"Not possible. You gave me everything I ever dreamed of, kids...one you carried when I couldn't."

"I loved being pregnant. It wasn't safe for you to do it. So, I carried your egg, and we made a beautiful and snarky, assertive young woman."

"All our kids are beautiful and snarky. I think your genetics bled in."

"That was kind of a backhanded compliment." She pinched my small love handle.

"But even better, we have a fairytale to tell the grandkids."

"We're grandparents." She huffed playfully.

"You're an extremely sexy grandma." I rubbed the softness of her lower belly that was covered with a few more stretch marks.

"If you make a GILF joke, I will put you on the couch."

"You like me waking you up giving you head way too much to put me on the couch." I smirked as she groaned, and I cupped her right breast, lifted it from where it had sagged and leaned over her to suck at the hard peak, and repeated on the other. "And you wouldn't do that to me. I get to wake up to a gorgeous woman in my bed every day for the rest of my life."

"You still think so after all these years?"

"Well, let's see." I tipped my head to the side. "Morning sex. Lunch-time office sex. Quickies before dinner. And, oh, at least once more before we go to sleep. Like I told you twenty years ago, I created monster. And what's better than my baby-girl in my arms whether we fuck or not?"

"I love you, Dani."

"I love you, too, Odessa. I just hope I loved you enough."

"You loved me until there was no room for sadness or pain. Like we always said, just you and our kids, the rest was just me waiting for the time my happily ever after showed up."

She lifted her head and brushed her lips to mind, and I grabbed her hip to turn her toward me. It was just us, and it's all I'd ever wanted.

About the Author

Siobhan Smile is an author of happily ever afters with a twist. They features characters of all sizes, shapes, sexualities, gender identities and races. Reading a Siobhan Smile book lets you escape for a few hours whether that is to an alien world or a contemporary setting, you'll find something outside the norm. Writing books for Siobhan is more than simply telling a story, it's a way for everyone to see themselves get a HEA.

Author Pronouns: Nonbinary/Gender Nonconforming - They/Them

Also by Siobhan Smile

Writing As J. M. Dabney

Executioners Series

Ghost

Joker

King

Sin & Saint

Trenton Security

Livingston

Little

Gage

Pure

Masiello Brothers

The Taming of Violet

3 Moments Trilogy

A Matter of Time

The Men of Canter Handyman

Black Leather & Knuckle Tattoos

Chance at the Impossible

Bloody Knuckles Bar & Grill

Clipping the Gargoyle's Wings

Standalone

By Way of Pain (Criminal Delights - Assassins)

Christmas, Bloody Christmas (By Way of Pain Xmas Story)

Waited So Long

An Odd, Little Girl

Claiming Whisper

Adoring Beast

A Yuri Sorenson Mystery

Not Another Statistic

Permanent Freebies

Has the Honeymoon Ended? (Brawlers Short Valentine's Story)

Once Upon a Bear Claw

The Scars She Bears (Executioners Short)